Asoka's Secret

notionpress.com

Asoka's Secret

ASH KING

notionpress.com

Notion Press

Old No. 38, New No. 6

McNichols Road, Chetpet

Chennai - 600 031

First Published by Notion Press 2015

ISBN: 978-93-5206-279-9

MAURYAN KINGDOM : 270 BC

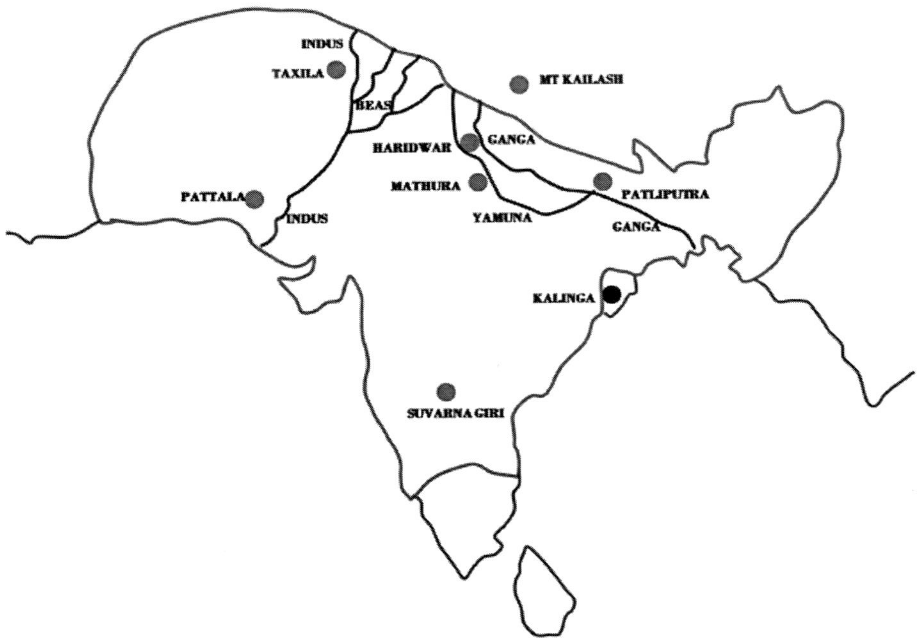

ROUTE OF KAILASH MANSAROVAR YATRA EX DELHI

1

The Battle of Kalinga (261 BC)

It was a dark and humid summer noon. The thick jungle seemed to envelope all signs of life within its fold. Far away on the horizon, the battle field lay strewn with rotten and decaying corpses. There was hardly any sound. It seemed as if the whole world had suddenly been annihilated leaving only *Asoka* to witness the devastation.

From as far as the gaze would travel, there were piles and piles of corpses. The *Daya* river had turned crimson red from the blood of fallen soldiers and animals, while the final lights of the day were faintly illuminating the full spectrum of death and destruction caused by the terrible battle. The warriors of *Kalinga* had fought with a ferocity never witnessed before. Like an army possessed and filled with death wish, they kept on charging against the mighty and superior *Mauryan* army. The neat line of archers with their deadly poison tipped arrows waited patiently with their taunt bows for the *Kalingan* warriors to come within striking distance. *Aakraman* (Attack), the *Senapati* (Chief) bellowed and out flew the arrows from the bows like a hail of iron raining down from the skies. The *Mauryan* army were well trained and better equipped. There was hardly any match. They prided themselves for their superior fighting skill and stratagem, which had resulted in their Empire extending from the *Hindu Kush* Mountain in the west to the plains of *Brahmaputra* in the east and the *Deccan* plateau towards the south. *Kalinga*, like a stub born child had refused to come under the *Mauryan* flag and was paying the price for its pride and arrogance. *Chanakya* had trained and equipped the *Mauryans* well.

What the *Kalingans* lacked in numbers, weapons and tactics, they more than made up in their will, courage and determination to fight. Loss was not an option. They had decided from the beginning that they will fight till the end and make sure that the *Mauryans* pay the price for their misadventure. The *Kalingans* were aware of the might of the *Mauryans*, but also knew that it was no match against their tenacity, pride and determination, which coursed through their veins.

The *Mauryan* army led by King *Asoka* had over three hundred thousand infantry, ten thousand cavalry and a thousand war elephants. The *Kalingan* army was led by *Rani* (Queen) *Padmavati* with a hundred thousand infantry, one thousand cavalry and three hundred war elephants. The *Kalingans* fought a fair and just war based on the principles of *Dharam Yudh* (Religious war) while the *Mauryans* fought according to the age old strategy devised by their first prime minister *Chanakya*, which was based on adopting a course of action according to the terrain, enemy, motives and a host of other factors with the single purpose of winning war at any cost or a war by all means, the *Kut Yudh* (Devious war).

The war had begun in the eighth year after *Asoka* had assumed the throne of the mighty *Mauryan* Empire. Since the time of *Asoka*'s grandfather, the mighty *Chandragupta Maurya*, *Kalinga* had defied the *Mauryan* Empire's advances and had continued to remain an independent entity. The war with *Kalinga* was more a matter of political compulsions and personal prestige than an actual need for expanding territory. *Asoka* had to prove to his people that he was the *Maha Samrat* (King of Kings) or *Asoka the Great*, the invincible one.

The *Mauryan* army had adopted the lotus battle formation with *Asoka* and the *Senapati* at the center with the remaining force spread across two wings and two flanks like a lotus flower in full bloom. Each petal of the formation was organized under the Vice Chief or *Up Senapati* and had rows of foot soldiers, archers, charioteers and war elephants arranged in depth. The archers were utilized to break the rank and file of the assault much before it could reach the main body, while the cavalry was utilized as a maneuver element to attack from the flanks. The war elephants were a terrifying sight to watch with their full body armor and huge ivory tusks. Each of the elephants had three soldiers with long javelins, bows and arrows mounted on it and were used to cause panic and havoc in the enemy ranks by charging into the defenses and scattering the neat rows of archers, charioteers and soldiers. The elephants were made to drink intoxicants and country liquor before the battle to make them fierce and uncontrollable. Sometimes, they became so uncontrollable that they would turn around and run over their own army crushing anyone who came in their way.

Rani Padmavati had organized her army in the traditional battle formation of defense in depth. Her chief had approached her and warned her of the consequences of an open conflict with the *Mauryans*. Now is not the right time to take on the mighty *Mauryan* army, he said. We are greatly outnumbered and defeat is almost certain. *Asoka* has come well prepared and will only stop once we unconditionally surrender before him, he added. If we want to see the rising sun and our families, then we need to surrender to *Asoka* and avoid the blood bath that is inevitable to follow.

The young princess was in a dilemma. On one hand was the life and safety of her citizens, who had marched alongside her in the face of certain death; while on the other lay defeat and humiliation. The burden of living a life of captivity without free will and freedom was too difficult to bear. The reason that the *Mauryans* had never been able to conquer *Kalinga* was because they had never compromised on their freedom. The chief waited for the princess to make up her mind and pronounce her decision. Like a true soldier he had put forth facts and assessment in a simple and lucid manner. He was not afraid of death. In his profession it was considered an honor to die in battle fighting valiantly and courageously against the oppressors of his motherland. Finally, the princess made up her mind. She summoned the chief and expressed her desire to address all the soldiers prior to the battle. Valiant soldiers of *Kalinga*, she began. It is indeed an honor for me to lead such a brave and courageous lot of men into battle. I am aware that we leave behind our aged, women and children who wait anxiously for our return. There comes a time in life when one has to choose between life and freedom, between honor and subservience, between pride and slavery. Our ancestors had never succumbed to pressures of life and death and never compromised on our cherished values and freedom, and neither would I. Tomorrow is our day of reckoning. We will teach the villain *Asoka* and his army such a lesson that for the next hundred generations he will never dare to set his dirty feet on our sacred land. Show the *Mauryan* army what a true *Kalingan* is capable of. Let there be so much bloodshed on the battle field that the *Daya* river's color changes from blue to red.

The battle of *Kalinga* lasted for fourteen days. The fighting was so intense and fierce that it is remembered as one of the bloodiest battles ever fought in the history of mankind. The entire *Kalingan* army was wiped out with more than a hundred thousand soldiers killed. Almost an equal number of *Mauryan* soldiers also died. The battle field was littered with limbs and carcasses of men, horses and elephants. The stench was unbearable and overpowering. Amongst all this, *Asoka* stood on the nearby *Dhauli* hills and surveyed the battlefield. A deep sense of guilt and sadness over powered him. What have I done, he cried with hands outstretched towards heavens, begging for mercy. A surge of grief overtook him and he fell down motionless on the ground. The seed of today's battle were sown by his grandfather, the great king *Chandragupta Maurya*.

Chandragupta Maurya

In 340 BC, *Chandragupta* was born to *Mura*, a *shudra* (Untouchable) lady of humble decent, out of wedlock, as a result of a tempestuous affair between her and *Nanda* prince *Sarvarthasiddi*. Since childhood, *Chandragupta* had developed an intense hatred against his father and the *Nanda* dynasty. He was daily ridiculed and made fun of by the children of his age and his mother was looked down upon by the society. His hatred reached a peak when his father refused to recognize him and his mother in public and threw them out of the royal court. From that day onwards, *Chandragupta* vowed that he would not rest in peace till the time he had not overthrown the *Nandas* and killed his father. Anger and hatred sometimes brings out extreme qualities in a person. Such was the burning desire in *Chandragupta* to become the king and overthrow the *Nandas* that he was ready to go to any extreme to achieve his goal. He was sharp, intelligent, brave and courageous, and possessed exceptional leadership qualities. He managed to win over support from a sizeable number of disgruntled youth and formed a rag tag army. All he needed now was an intelligent Prime Minister to help him fulfill his life's mission.

The *Nanda* rule originated from *Magdha* (ancient Indian state) during the 4th and 5th century BC. At its peak, the Empire extended from *Bengal* in the east to

Punjab in the west and *Vindhyas* to the south. It was founded by *Mahapadma Nanda* who was born to a *shudra* mother and being of low descent was humiliated and oppressed during his childhood; the scars of which he carried throughout his life. The *Nandas* had a huge army consisting of two hundred thousand infantry, twenty thousand cavalry, two thousand charioteers and three thousand war elephants. *Mahapadma Nanda* died at the ripe age of 88 years and was able to provide stability to the *Nanda* Empire. He ruled with an iron fist and had a deep hatred against the higher castes and priests. He used to often humiliate and make fun of them. Most of the upper caste persons and *Brahmins* (Priests) lived a life of penury under him. *Mahapadma* was survived by his son *Dhan Nanda*. He was an evil and atrocious man who lived a life full of vice, deceit and treachery. He levied exorbitant taxes, looted and plundered the common man, abused his ministers and murdered anyone who opposed him.

In 326 BC, *Alexander* invaded India. In the epic battle of *Hydaspes* (Present day *Beas* river), he defeated the Indian king *Porus*, but was so impressed with his courage that he made him a Satrap. For the first time in history, two major Empires, the *Nanda* and *Macedonian* shared a common land border. However, the Roman Empire which had won almost half the world were reluctant to cross the *Ganga* river as they had heard tales about the ferocity and courage of the *Nanda* warriors and were terrified of its army of war elephants.

Takshshila was a flourishing international university during the fourth century BC. It was situated in the ancient city of *Taxila* and connected to *Patliputra*

(Capital city of *Nanda* Empire) by *Uttarapatha*, the northern highway of commerce. The university had foreign students from *Greece, Persia, Babylon* and *China*. It taught a host of disciplines including engineering, medicine, art, political science, economy and occult. *Chanakya* was an eminent professor of economics and political science at the university.

Sakatala, a *brahmin* was a minister in the court of *Dhana Nanda* and was time and again humiliated by the king. *Dhana Nanda* took a liking for *Sakatala*'s wife. To keep *Sakatala* away from the capital, *Dhana Nanda* sent him to *Takshshila* to study state craft under *Chanakya* and in his absence abducted his wife and forcibly made her his slave. The pious lady could not tolerate the humiliation and shame of becoming the king's keep and self-immolated herself in the presence of the entire court. The news of his wife's tragic end reached *Sakatala* after a few months at *Takshshila*. He was devastated and shattered. He vowed that he would not sleep till he had brought about the downfall of the Nanda dynasty and avenged the death of his beloved wife.

Sakatala knew that *Chanakya* was a master of state craft and politics and had the intellect to engineer the downfall of the *Nanda* rule. He also knew that *Chanakya* was a highly respected *brahmin* and was worshipped by the pupil and academic community at *Takshshila*. He somehow persuaded *Chanakya* to accompany him to *Patliputra* and attend the royal court of *Dhana Nanda*. *Chanakya* was hesitant in the beginning to undertake such a long and arduous journey but gave in finally to the continuous persuasions of *Sakatala*. On reaching the royal court in *Patliputra, Sakatala* introduced *Chanakya* as an upper class *brahmin* who was well versed in all scriptures and was a master of politics and state craft. *Dhana Nanda* gathered the impression that *Sakatala* was taunting him in front of the entire court by making him realize that he was of low descent and a progeny of *shudra* caste while *Chanakya* was of a superior caste. The king lost his temper and ordered his soldiers to disrobe both *Chanakya* and *Sakatala*, whip them and then parade them naked with blackened faces mounted backwards on donkeys across the entire city of *Patliputra*. *Chanakya* was livid and seething with rage on the humiliation that he had to suffer at the hands of *Dhana Nanda*. He untied his *choti* (sacred knot of hair) and pledged that he will not tie it again until he had brought about the downfall of the *Nanda* Empire. The plan of *Sakatala* had worked.

On reaching *Takshshila*, *Chanakya* started planning the downfall of the *Nanda* Empire. He started searching for a potential leader who had the same hatred which he had against the *Nanda* Empire. *Chandragupta Maurya* at that time was trying to forge an alliance with *Porus* in order to collectively fight against the Nandas. But, the alliance failed and did not work out. *Chandragupta Maurya* stopped at *Taxila* for a few days on his way back to *Patliputra*. There, he was introduced to *Chanakya* by *Sakatala*, and the rest, as they say, is history. It was an ideal win – win situation. Both *Chandragupta Maurya* and *Chanakya* were consumed by their collective hatred against *Dhan Nanda* and complemented each other in more than one ways. What *Chandragupta Maurya* possessed in terms of courage and valor, *Chanakya* possessed in intellect and vision.

Chanakya knew that *Chandragupta* required a well-trained and large army in case he needed to take on *Dhan Nanda*. He also ruled out a direct confrontation with the *Nandas* as it would result in a lot of blood shed with no guarantee of a sure shot win. The armies of that era fought a predictable battle. A battle field was decided and the two opposing sides met there. The battle used to rage from morning to dusk and the evening and night were spent in respective camps tending to the dead and wounded and preparing for the next day's battle. *Chanakya* changed the rules of the game. He formulated and perfected the strategy of *kut yudh* or devious warfare. In this kind of warfare, the ultimate aim was victory and the only rule applicable was that there were no rules. Here, everything was permitted. This type of warfare was preferred when there was great disparity amongst the opposing sides. The concept of weapons too underwent a paradigm change. Information, deception, knowledge, guile, cunningness and deceit were all different types of weapons. The aim was to attack the enemy when he was the least prepared and at the most unexpected time and place. The traditional boundaries of friends and foes, war and peace, time and space got blurred. Who was friend and who enemy was never known. Intent was a closely guarded secret and the type of situation decided on the type of friendship. The mind of the commander became the real target. Battles no longer were fought at the battlefields but were waged simultaneously in different places, at all the times. A great emphasis was laid on espionage and spying. A spy was considered to be a force multiplier and the biggest asset to the state. Everyone and everything were to be observed and reported.

The first step towards their victory over *Dhan Nanda* was to keep their intent a closely guarded secret.

Chandragupta Maurya enrolled himself at the *Takshshila* University and sent his followers back to Patliputra. *Chanakya* did not discuss the events that took place at the royal court with anyone and continued to teach at Takshshila. *Chanakya* and *Chandragupta* met each other in secret and started cultivating spies. The spies were given specific tasks and information was shared strictly on a need to know basis. The first breakthrough came when *Chandragupta* was successful in planting a spy in the court of *Dhana Nanda*.

Slowly, *Chanakya* and *Chandragupta* were able to infiltrate spies into the *Nanda* army and various departments in the kingdom. The spies were continuously gathering and updating information on all the activities and plans of the Nanda Empire. A detailed list of key and important functionaries and their vices and weaknesses was prepared.

Chanakya had realized the importance of propaganda in influencing the minds of the local populace. He was aware that *Taxila* was situated at the periphery of the *Nanda* Empire and was weakly influenced by the central policy and administration emanating from the central government at *Patliputra*. He and *Chandragupta* put an elaborate propaganda plan into place. *Chandragupta* used to frequent markets, liquor and prostitution houses and hold large number of informal meetings with the disgruntled youth. Subsequently, the spies used to spread a disinformation campaign and create the impression in the minds of the populace that *Chandragupta* was a superior being and capable of performing miracles. He had been sent by heavens to overthrow the tyrant rule of *Dhan Nanda* and create a just and righteous Empire. All those who would enroll in *Chandragupta*'s army would be the chosen ones and will possess the strength of ten elephants and hundred lions. Rumors were spread of *Chandragupta* performing miracles and bringing dead people back to life.

Slowly the ranks of *Chandragupta*'s army swelled. With the help of *Chanakya*, *Chandragupta* was able to persuade king *Porus* to forge an alliance with him. Meanwhile, the army of spies which had infiltrated into the entire rank and file of the *Nanda* army was rising up in the chain of hierarchy. Many of them were in senior positions and ensured that the news coming in from *Taxila* was suitably filtered and no word regarding the brewing rebellion in the periphery of the kingdom reached the king's ears. *Dhan Nanda* only got to hear what *Chanakya* wanted him to hear.

The army of *Chandragupta* with the external support of King *Porus* started capturing territory at the fringes of the *Nanda* Empire. Based on the advice of *Chanakya*, *Chandragupta* ensured that the local populace of captured territory were not troubled and allowed to continue with their day to day affairs. Moreover, an efficient and effective administrative machinery was put in place that not only ensured that the local community including farmers, artisans and traders were not troubled but also an atmosphere of peace and tranquility prevailed where persons could prosper without fear of thieves, bandits and external aggression. The populist measures implemented in the captured territory ensured that local able bodied youth were more than willing to enroll in the *Mauryan* army. *Chanakya*'s extensive network of spies made sure that *Dhan Nanda* remained clueless and in a state of oblivion about the actual happenings of his Empire till it became too late to do anything about it.

Dhan Nanda was completely taken by surprise when he discovered that the *Mauryan* army had reached the outskirts of *Patliputra*. In a fit of rage he ordered the beheading of the messenger who came to the court with the news of the invasion. He immediately asked his chief to prepare for an offensive. The infiltrated *Mauryan* army of spies swung into action. The royal armory suddenly got torched and a third of the *Nanda* weapons got destroyed even before they could be made to bear against the *Mauryan* army. There were reports of food poisoning in the army's cook houses with a large number of soldiers falling sick. A number of rumors started flowing about the super natural powers of *Chandragupta* raising alarm and panic within the ranks of the *Nanda* army. Some war elephants were fed *bhang*, a local intoxicant, mixed with their food, as a result of which they became uncontrollable and crushed their own *mahouts*. Eventually when both the armies faced each other, it was clearly evident that the Nanda's were staring at defeat. The strong and mighty *Nanda* army which had instilled fear in *Alexander's* army was no longer there. What was present on the battle field was a disjoint body of troops under poor leadership having low morale. Everybody was waiting to run away from the battlefield or join ranks with the *Mauryan* army at the first opportunity.

The *Mauryan* army under *Chandragupta* won the battle easily without much bloodshed. The *Nandas* were no match against the astute leadership of *Chandragupta* and great intellect of *Chanakya*. *Dhan Nanda* and *Sarvathasiddhi* were killed in battle. The entire *Nanda* Empire came under *Mauryan* rule. For the first time in history, a person with no inherited kingdom or army was able to defeat the largest Empire in the Indian subcontinent. *Chandragupta* and *Chanakya* had achieved their aim. In a splendid ceremony attended by a large number of neighboring kings, *Chandragupta Maurya* was appointed the king with the title of *Maha Samrat* (Great King) with *Chanakya* as his Prime Minister.

The *Mauryan* Empire under *Chandragupta Maurya* represented a golden period in India's history. The Empire was expanded and consolidated. *Chanakya* proved to be one of the finest and ablest Prime Ministers of all times. He nurtured no political ambitions and was loyal towards the king and the Empire. His focus was on administration and security. A number of reforms were initiated in the administration of the kingdom including transparent taxation system, accounting of land holdings, policing and infrastructure building. An elaborate system of secret policing was put into place with spies spread across the entire length and breadth of the *Mauryan* kingdom. Spies were even infiltrated into the neighboring kingdoms and no one was above the gaze of *Chanakya*'s secret police. He even had a group of trusted spies to monitor the activities of the king. A strong defense and information network, transparency in public dealing and effective administration were the cornerstones of the *Mauryan* Empire. *Chanakya* too had his share of enemies because of his proximity and strong hold over the king. Most of them were amongst the king's council of ministers, waiting patiently for an opportunity to stab *Chanakya* in the back.

As part of his consolidation strategy, *Chandragupta* conquered most of the *Alexander's* satraps adjoining the *Mauryan* Empire in the west. In an alliance with *Seluceus Necator*, he gifted him five hundred war elephants and married his beautiful daughter *Durdhara*. *Megasthenese* was sent as an envoy to *Patliputra* during this time.

Chanakya was always concerned that *Chandragupta* could be poisoned by one of his rivals. Being a person well versed in ancient medicine, he started secretly adding small doses of poison in *Chandragupta*'s food to slowly build up his immunity. Over a period of time, *Chandragupta* could ingest large quantities of poison with ease, which otherwise could prove fatal to a normal human being. One day when *Chandragupta* was relishing his food in the presence of queen *Durdhara*, he asked her to join him. The moment the queen took the first morsel in her mouth, she started choking. *Chanakya* who was in the vicinity, immediately realized what had happened. In order to save the child in her womb, he slit the queen's throat before she could ingest the poisonous food and thereafter cut open the womb and saved the child. In this process, a drop of poison touched the young child's forehead and formed a scar. The king watched the entire scene helplessly and could do nothing to save his queen. The king's new born son was named *Bindusara* or the one with a mark on forehead. *Bindusara* would later succeed *Chandragupta* as the king.

Bindusara Maurya

At the age of forty two, *Chandragupta Maurya* handed over the reins of the Mauryan Empire to *Bindusara* and as per *Jain* customs went on a pilgrimage to southern India. *Bindusara* at that time was twenty two years old. *Chandragupta* never returned to the *Mauryan* kingdom and shortly afterwards voluntarily gave up eating and drinking and died.

Chanakya continued to be the Prime Minister to *Bindusara*. The Mauryan Empire further flourished and consolidated under *Bindusara*. He was a just, kind and considerate ruler. Barring the *Chola*, *Pandya* and *Chera* kingdom to the south and *Kalinga* in south east, the *Mauryan* Empire ruled over the entire peninsular India. It was known as the Empire that ruled over the land between both the seas, i.e. the Bay of *Bengal* towards the east and the *Arabian* Sea towards the west. *Bindusara* had sixteen wives which bore him a hundred and one children. Amongst his sons, *Sumana* was the eldest and *Tissa* the youngest. *Asoka* was the son of *Dhammi*, who was one of *Bindusara*'s favorite queens.

One of the major achievements of *Bindusara* was building highways of peace, friendship and trade with far away distant lands. The Silk route and *Khyber* Pass trade routes were established during his times. Trade was carried out with *Tibet*, *China*, Middle East and *Hellenic* Empires. *Asoka* was a courageous and ambitious son of *Bindusara*. *Sumana* was made the governor of *Taxila* while *Asoka* was made the governor of *Ujjain* (Ancient Indian City).

Subandhu was one of the ministers in *Bindusara*'s kingdom. He nursed a secret desire of overthrowing *Chanakya* and becoming the Prime Minister. He knew that *Chanakya* maintained an army of spies and would deal with him severely in case he came to know about his intentions. Therefore, *Subandhu* maintained a very cordial relationship with *Chanakya* and waited patiently for an opportune moment to strike. In a very subtle manner, he started winning the trust of *Bindusara*. He was cautious to ensure that his overtures with the king do not raise any suspicion and used time as a weapon to slowly poison the king against *Chanakya*. Once, when *Chanakya* had gone on a pilgrimage, *Subandhu* revealed to the king the circumstances of his birth. He poisoned his mind and told him that *Chanakya* was the one responsible for the murder of *Bindusara*'s mother. *Bindusara* was filled with intense rage. He immediately summoned *Chanakya* back from the pilgrimage and confronted him.

Chanakya, being a proud man, became angry when he was spoken to in a derogatory manner by the king. He walked out of the royal kingdom and sat down on a heap of dung placed in the centre of the market place. *Chanakya* vowed that he will go on an indefinite hunger strike and will die in front of the entire citizens in protest against the king's treatment to him. There was outrage amongst the citizens of *Patliputra* when the saw their Prime Minister being treated in such a shoddy and derogatory manner. The news of *Chanakya*'s fast reached all corners of the Empire and there was widespread anger against the actions of the king.

A number of ministers and governors met king *Bindusara* and revealed the nefarious designs of *Subandhu*. They advised him to personally meet *Chanakya* and request him to take back his pledge of indefinite fast unto death. *Bindusara* called *Subandhu* and ordered him to go and ask *Chanakya* for forgiveness or else he would be publicly executed at the square where *Chanakya* was on indefinite fast. *Subandhu* hid a burning ember in his *Kamandal* (water jug used for spiritual practices) and went up to the heap of dung where *Chanakya* was fasting. In front of the gathered crowd, he asked *Chanakya* for forgiveness and moved forward to touch his feet with his forehead as a mark of respect. When *Subandhu* bent down to touch *Chanakya*'s feet, he removed the burning ember from his *Kamandal* and slid it underneath the dry dung. The heap of dung immediately caught fire. *Subandhu* gripped *Chanakya* in a death vice on the burning heap of dung from where huge flames of fire started rising. *Chanakya*, who had grown weak from fasting was unable to escape from the death grip of *Subandhu* and both *Chanakya* and *Subandhu* died in the fire as helpless citizens kept on watching in disbelief, shock and panic.

In the meantime, *Asoka's* clout as an administrator and a fearless warrior was growing. A revolt had brewed up in *Taxila* due to high handedness of *Sumana* and *Asoka* was dispatched from *Ujjain* to quell the disturbance. After sorting out the matter at *Taxila*, *Asoka* returned to *Patliputra*. News of his courage and sharp acumen had spread far and wide and he was considered the most worthy of occupying the *Mauryan* Empire.

Bindusara fell seriously ill at the age of forty eight. As he lay on his deathbed, a war of succession broke out amongst his sons. *Asoka* was in *Patliputra* at that time. He gathered his followers and went on a gory rampage killing his ninety nine brothers and leaving only the youngest *Tissa* alive. *Asoka* seized power and became the third king of the *Mauryan* Empire. Everyone shivered.

Asoka

Asoka was thirty six years old when he became the king. He immediately started consolidating his hold over the Empire. The battle of *Kalinga* made him realize the futility of war and conquest. He became a changed man after the war and vowed never to hurt anyone anymore. In fact, he went a step further and assumed the responsibility of protecting everyone's life and freedom, whether they belonged to his kingdom or otherwise. He became a *Buddhist* and propagated the religion far and wide. For the rest of his life, *Asoka* administered the *Mauryan* Empire in an effective and efficient manner which ensured that citizens lived a life of peace, prosperity and dignity. Art and culture flourished. Progress was made in all spheres of life and visitors from far and wide came to *Taxila*, *Ujjain* and *Patliputra* to witness the change under *Asoka*.

This was the time when it all started. Saying this, the old man stood up from the floor of the cave and proceeded to light the earthen lamp which was slowly extinguishing due to lack of oil. Barring the earthen lamp and a deer skin rug on the floor, there was no material thing inside the cave. It was snowing outside and the temperature inside was freezing, but the old man was bare chested wearing only a loin cloth to cover his private parts and appeared to be immune to the vagaries of nature. A strange sense of wellness and calm enveloped him and his entire surroundings. Time stood still and *John* realized that his search was about to come to an end. He will get the answers to the questions that were tormenting him in his dreams every single day since he was a child.

2

John was born on 03 Jan 1993 to *Andrew* and *Shiela Smith* in San Jose, California. Both *Andrew* and *Shiela* were freelance software developers who had met during an online gaming competition and had fallen head over heels over each other. Marriage followed after six months of fast paced dating. In spite of *Andrew* and *Shiela* coming from different backgrounds and parts of the world; *Andrew* was a hardcore fifth generation American while *Shiela* was a staunch *Hindu* from India, it seemed as if the marriage was made in heaven and the couple were made for each other. *Andrew* and *Shiela* complimented each other. Not only were they in the same profession but they also shared the same tastes and hobbies. *Andrew*'s parents welcomed *Shiela* with open arms and the couple settled down to day to day living after the initial excitement of the marriage weaned off. Things were not so smooth with *Shiela*'s parents. *Shiela* belonged to a high caste *Brahmin* (*Hindu* priest upper caste) family of Allahabad and her father was the head priest of the local *Hindu* temple. Her parents had always nurtured a strong desire that she should get married into a respectable *brahmin* family like theirs.

Shiela's parents were left with no choice but to accept the couple when they heard the news of *Shiela*'s pregnancy. The old parents were overjoyed when *Shiela* took *John* and *Andrew* to Allahabad to meet them. As part of family ritual, *John*'s head was tonsured and the sacred thread *janeu* tied around his waist. A large number of family and friends were called for the customary naming ceremony where *John*'s horoscope was prepared and his Indian name decided. *Shiela*'s father was taken aback when he read *John*'s horoscope which prophesized that he would be a monk and leave his family at the age of twenty, never to come back.

John had an uneventful childhood. He was average in studies and sports and mingled around freely with everyone. Occasionally, every two to three years, the family would visit Shiela's parents in Allahabad. Allahabad is one of the ancient Indian cities dating back its existence to several millennia. During *Vedic* era(1750–500 BC), the city was known as *Prayag* or the confluence of three holy rivers, *Ganga*, *Yamuna* and *Saraswati*. It is one of the most sacred *Hindu* pilgrimage centre and one of the four locations of *Kumbh Mela*, a religious gathering which is the largest human gathering in the world.

When *John* was seventeen, the family went to Allahabad during their usual annual visit to India. The visit marked the beginning of a series of strange experiences which started haunting *John*. One day, as *John* was walking towards the *ghat* (Bank) of river *Ganga*, he was stopped by a naked *sadhu* (follower of an ancient Indian religious sect). The *sadhu* looked at him and started laughing. *John* was taken aback. So now you have come as a white man, the *sadhu* said in a deep throated voice. You might try your best to run away from your destiny, but fate will not allow you to escape. You may change gender, race and appearances over different births but the soul will remain the same. I see you clearly, my friend *bhikshu* (Indian monk). Ditch these fancy clothes and come with me to the *Himalayas*, like last time, the *sadhu* said. *John* broke into a sweat and started running towards home as fast as his legs could carry him.

On reaching home, *John* narrated the entire episode to his parents and grandfather. *Andrew* got perturbed and wanted to take the first flight out of India. He was not much of a religious guy and did not believe in reincarnation and rebirth. *Shiela* though having strong *Hindu* linkages hardly took these things seriously. Must be a crack man under the influence of *charas* (Indian local hemp often used as a cheap intoxicant by *sadhus*), she said. Let's not take this incident too seriously. Her father became quiet. He knew that *John*'s horoscope had predicted that he would become a monk and now this holy man was addressing *John* as if he knew him from his previous birth.

The rest of the stay at Allahabad was uneventful and the family returned to San Jose. Though everything looked normal from outside but deep inside *John* was very disturbed. The words of the *sadhu* kept troubling him. He did not want to worry his parents so kept his thoughts to himself. What if what the *sadhu* said was true, he thought.

Then, the dream started. The same dream every night. The entire battle of Kalinga was played and replayed in John's dreams, always waking him up drenched in sweat and shivering with fear. Once, John dreamt of seeing a clear blue sky, towering snowcapped mountains, a crystal clear huge lake, total stillness and a continuous chant of *come to me, come to me...* He experienced a strange feeling of inner peace and calm during the dream as if he needed to follow it in order to fulfill some unfinished business.

John decided to act on the dream. Like a detective he would try to find out the location of the lake by the mountain side which had appeared in his dream. In case, a message was being conveyed to him, then he will decipher it. After all, he wanted to get to the bottom of this and stop the nightmares which were constantly troubling him. Since, the naked *sadhu* at Allahabad mentioned that he was a monk, then in all probability the location in the dream must be somewhere in the Himalayas. But where, was the big question, which he wanted to answer.

The Himalayas are twenty four hundred kilometers long mountain ranges that separate the great Tibetan plateau from the Indian subcontinent. There are over a hundred mountain peaks above seven thousand meters including the world's highest peak *Mount Everest*. The other major peaks are *K2*, *Kanchenjanga* and *Lohotse* which have been formed by the collision of the *Indian Tectonic Plate* with the *Eurasian Plate.* The *Himalayas* run along the west – northwest to east – southeast direction. The world's three major river basins, *Indus*, *Ganges* and *Tsangpo* (*Bhramaputra* in India) originate from the *Himalayas*. For centuries, *Himalayas* have been considered the sacred abode of Gods and saints and worshipped by both the *Hindus* and *Buddhists*.

The Tibetan plateau is also known as the roof of the world or the third pole. Its average altitude is one thousand six hundred meters and the world's biggest water basins and mountain peaks originate from this plateau. The plateau is a vast barren desolate plain which spreads out like a never ending canvas in all directions. There are a number of ancient passes and routes which join the Tibetan plateau with the plains of India and Trans *Himalayan* interaction and trade was quite common in ancient times.

There are more than five thousand high altitude lakes in the *Himalayan – Tibet* region. Which one of them was the lake which came in *John*'s dream was a million dollar question which he intended to answer. The lake which he saw in his dream was very vast and stretched for miles together. Its water was crystal clear and turquoise blue. The sight of the majestic lake surrounded by snowcapped mountains on all sides was so breathtaking and livid that he knew that he would be able to recognize it in the first instance. Thanks to the internet, *John* was able to home on to the lake of his dream in a matter of few days. The lake in his dream was positively the *Kailash Mansarovar*.

The *Kailash Mansarovar* is one of the most sacred lakes in *Hindu*, *Buddhist* and *Jain* religion. Located at a height of over fifteen thousand feet above mean sea level, the lake is circular in shape with a circumference of eighty eight Km. Surprisingly, it is a fresh water lake in a region surrounded by salt water lakes. To the north of the lake is the majestic *Mount Kailash* and to its east is lake *Rakshasthal* (place for defense). In Tibet, the lake is referred to as *Mapam Yumko*. For thousands of years, the *Hindus* have believed that *Mansarovar* is the origin of the four mighty rivers of *Himalayas*; *Brahmaputra*, *Karnali*, *Sutlej* and *Indus*. It is believed that whoever takes a bath in the holy river and drinks its water will be freed of all his present and past sins. *Hindus* believe that the lake was first created in the mind of *Brahma* (Hindu God of creation) and hence its name as *Man* (mind) *Sarovar* (lake). *Mount Kailash* is believed to be the abode of Lord *Shiva*, the *Hindu* God associated with death and destructions. The lake is also believed to be the summer abode of swans, the celestial vehicle of *Lord Brahma*. Buddhists believe that *Buddha* was mystically conceived while his mother was bathing in the lake.

John decided to visit Lake *Mansarovar* in pursuit of his dream. The dream was now occurring more frequently, as if there was a hidden urgency and an important message which someone was trying to convey to him. At the first opportunity, *John* got himself registered with the Indian government's summer tour to the *Mansarovar* Lake.

The journey to *Mansarovar* Lake starts from New Delhi and passes through scenic and quaint towns and villages en route. After night halts at *Almora*, *Chaukori*, *Dharchula*, *Sirkha*, *Gala*, *Budhi*, *Gunji* and *Nabhidhang*, the party entered China through *Lipulek* pass for their next phase of journey. The going became tiresome and hazardous as they passed through narrow tracks, landslide prone areas and high altitude terrain going through *Darchin*, *Deraphu*, *Zongrebu*, *Hore*, *Quju* and *Zaida* to finally reach the beautiful *Mansarovar* Lake and *Kailash Parbat* (mountain). The first sight of the magnificent lake and *Mount Kailash* left everyone spellbound and speechless. The travelers were filled with awe and forgot all about their pain and aches. Time stood still and the party totally mesmerized and unable to move. The guides who were accompanying the party and had watched the scene repeat each and every time, looked at each other and smiled.

The crystal clear water of the lake reflected perfectly the snowcapped peaks of the *Himalayas* surrounding it. *Mount Kailash* rose over all the other peaks as a huge majestic cone shaped rocky knob; an eternal protector to the magical *Mansarovar* Lake.

John had no words left to describe his feelings. He was standing face to face with the picture he had seen in his dream. The resemblance was so uncanny and true that there was not even an iota of doubt in his mind that *Mansarovar* was not the lake of his dream. He felt as if he belonged here and this was his real home. His life till now: his parents, friends and colleagues seemed to be a mere deception aimed at distracting him from his real purpose. *John* belonged here and he felt it in every cell of his being. He had reached home. There was no going back now.

According to *Hindu* spiritual belief, a person is to take a holy dip in the lake, drink its water and circumambulate *Mansarovar* in order to cleanse the self of all past and present sins. The *parikarma* or walk along the circumference can take seven to ten days depending on a person's fitness level and the available weather. Landslides, rains, chilblain, muscle cramps and foot sores are quite common and only a handful of travelers complete the entire *parikrama* on foot. The others take the help of porters, ponies and Land Cruisers to complete the journey.

From the lake, *Mount Kailash* appears to be quite near, whereas in reality it is eighty Km north of the lake. Both *Hindus* and *Buddhists* believe that the centre of the earth originates from *Mount Kailash*. There are eight monasteries along the circumference of the lake, depicting the eight spokes of the *Dharam Chakra* or wheels of action, with *Chu Gumpa* being the most famous of them all.

Welcome my son; the voice literally jolted *John* out of his stupor. He looked back startled to see the smiling face of an old *Buddhist* monk staring at him. Do you speak English, *John* asked, as the old man gave an impression that he had never moved beyond the confines of the lake. I speak all the languages, the monk replied. When you speak from the heart, you rarely need the assistance of words to convey your thoughts. Come, the monk said… we have a lot of distance to travel and it will be night in a few hours' time. *John* was surprised by the behavior of the monk. Here was a man whom he had met for the first time in his life but who spoke and behaved as if he knew him since ages and was almost commandeering him to break away from the tour party and follow him to an unknown destination in the middle of nowhere. Yet, the monk exuded so much warmth and compassion that it was impossible to disobey him. *John* started following him and soon they were heading on an unknown path away from the tour party and the lake. In this desolate place away from civilization, *John* had surrendered completely to a stranger whom he had met a few minutes ago and had taken the most momentous decision in his life. There was no turning back.

After crossing highway G 219 which runs from *Lhotze* to *Nagari*, the duo started moving towards the mountain range where *Mount Kailash* lay. As far as the eyes could see, there was not a single bird or animal in sight. The old monk was moving swiftly and silently and *John* was finding it difficult to keep pace with him. After walking for about two hours, the old man stopped at the base of a mountain. From here onwards, you have to move alone, he said. But, where do I go in this desolate place surrounded by high mountains and harsh weather, asked *John*. Son, the monk said, we come and leave this world alone. There are certain journeys which need to be travelled alone. You need not be afraid. The one who has summoned you will protect you and lead you to him. Saying this, the old monk turned back and was lost sight off after a few minutes.

Don't be afraid, an inner voice said. The voice was so clear and real that *John* could have sworn that it was coming from the mountains as there was not a soul in sight and he was all alone. It was getting dark and though the temperature was still a few degrees above zero, the relentless strong gusts of wind had drastically increased the wind chill factor. *John* started shivering. He looked around for a place where he could take shelter for the night as the temperature was dropping quickly and he needed to make arrangements ASAP. Come here the voice said. *John* looked up and saw a faint mountain trail running along the contours of the mountain and disappearing around the bend. He decided to follow his instinct and started moving along the trail. The darkness coupled with strong icy winds and exhaustion was taking its toll on *John* and progress was slow and time consuming. By the time he reached the bend, *John* was totally exhausted and it had become pitch dark. The moon was behind a thick cloud cover and the ambient light was very poor. Loneliness crept in and *John* for the first time started having doubts on his dream and instincts. What if everything was a figment of his imagination? Back home, everyone would be a very worried lot when news of his absence from the tour reached them. It was such a desolate place that he was dead sure that it would be near impossible to find him. A weak and tired *John* decided to give up. He sat down on the nearest rock, closed his eyes and waited for nature to put him to eternal sleep.

Don't sleep son, the voice said. It suddenly jolted *John* out of his slumber. He looked up and saw a faint glow emanating from a crack in the mountains. Come here now, the voice commanded. *John* was suddenly filled with so much warmth and energy that he felt that he could fly. All previous thoughts of doom and despair left him and he literally ran towards the glowing light. As he approached the source of light, *John* could make out the faint outline of a cave within the recesses of the mountain. Had there been no light or guidance, the cave would have been unnoticed even in broad daylight. He entered the cave on his knees as the opening was very narrow but suddenly it opened up wide into a vast chamber. At the far end of the cave, an old man sat in deep meditation totally naked with only a single loin cloth covering his entire body. A deep blue hue was emanating from his body. It was the same light which *John* had seen from the bend of the mountain. He became delirious and collapsed unconscious to the ground.

When *John* regained consciousness, he saw the old monk sitting cross legged at his usual place and a small light emanating from an earthen lamp filled with oil. Where am I and who are you, *John* asked. You must be famished, asked the old man. I will answer all your questions but you must eat something first. What will you like to have, the old man asked. *John* looked around. There was nothing whatsoever in the entire cave and here this naked man was asking him what he would prefer to have. *John* felt like laughing. How about a double crusted thin mozzarella pizza, he said almost bursting out with laughter. The old man smiled. He put his hand behind a pile of stones and pulled out a piping hot double crusted thin mozzarella pizza, box packed. *John*'s eyes literally popped out. Eat, the old man said and then we will talk. After having eaten the best pizza of his life, a wide eyed but satiated *John* sat down in front of the old man, eager to solve the mystery of his life. The adventure had just begun.

3

I am *Manu Rishi* (sage), the old man said. I do not talk but communicate through telepathy. What seems like words spoken to you is nothing but thoughts directed towards you over the ether. I have been the one who has been communicating with you all these years. But why me, asked *John*. Well to begin with, there is some unfinished business of your past life and some new tasks awaiting you. *John* was flabbergasted. What nonsense, he said. I don't believe in this mumbo jumbo story. Why should I trust you? Your apprehension is well founded, replied the old man. Let me narrate you certain events which happened thousands of years ago and have a direct bearing on you. Then, once I am finished, you can decide for yourself your future course of action. Seems to be a fair bargain, *John* replied. I want you to promise me that you will guide me back to safety in case I decide to go back, he added. Presently, you are in the safest place, *Manu Rishi* said. But, if you wish to go back to from where you came, then I promise that I will guide you back to your parent's home in California, the old monk replied. He then narrated the story of the *Mauryan* Empire and *Asoka*.

I still don't get it, said *John*. How am I related in the whole story which you have just narrated? Be patient, I have not finished yet, said the old monk. He then went into deep meditation and started speaking…

Takshshila was a highly developed university in which advanced research on a number of secret technologies and projects were being carried out. This research was a closely guarded secret, known only to a handful of persons. Special areas of the forest and nearby mountains were isolated and placed out of bounds which were guarded by multi-tiered security arrangements to keep out curious eyes and ears. The scientists and students carrying out the research could not leave the facility for the rest of their lives. Such was the code of conduct that no notes or documents of the research were kept and the entire methods and procedures were verbatim remembered and transferred through the word of mouth from master to pupil and so on and so forth. Generations of masters and pupils carried out research on secret topics in this manner with no physical evidence. Strange sights and sounds emanated from these forests and mountains and the local population were made to believe that these places were the haunt of evil spirits and unsafe for venturing into by human being. *Chanakya* was among the few professors of the university who were aware of these secret researches. Since, *Takshshila* was part of the *Mauryan* Empire, *Chanakya* through his means ensured that the research being carried out at *Takshshila* gained momentum and a large number of breakthroughs were made which could alter the entire course of mankind. *Chanakya* was acutely aware that in case the secret research fell in the wrong hands, then it had the power to wipe out civilizations. A need was felt to spread out the research teams to various parts of the world in complete secrecy and ensure that the discoveries made were safe from persons with evil intent. This was going to be the world's best kept secret.

Chanakya formed a total of nine teams. A grand strategy was crafted to ensure safe and clandestine exit and relocation of the teams to various parts of the world. In the first step, nine separate teams of men were sent to all corners of the world to discover safe, isolated and inaccessible locations which could not be visited by humans for centuries to come. The locations had to be so remote that they could be accessed only during a particular time of the year with the window of opportunity not to exceed a week. No one knew the purpose of this mission except *Chanakya*. It took almost a year for the teams to return. The team leaders were personally debriefed by *Chanakya* and barring one chosen guide, the rest of the team members were segregated and sent to different parts of the kingdom and kept in solitary confinement for the rest of their lives. The guide was also placed under solitary confinement in an undisclosed location. Thus, barring *Chanakya*, no one knew the entire plan of shifting the research teams.

Over the course of nine years, the nine teams were relocated to different locations. Each team was led by a master whose integrity and loyalty towards the kingdom and *Chanakya* were unquestionably. The master was sworn to secrecy and had no worldly family or possessions. His only purpose in life was the safety and furtherance of the research being carried out by his team. The master was in constant touch with *Chanakya* through the medium of astral travel, an ancient technique where in the soul deliberately leaves the body connected to it by a silver spiritual cord and travels in the astral plane, a spiritual dimension in which meetings between the soul takes place instantaneously, irrespective of the physical location of the persons. Most of the spiritual masters across the innumerable worlds use the medium of astral travel to interact with each other, the old monk said. *John*'s eyes were wide with astonishment but he was convinced by the words of the old monk and did not doubt them as he himself had eaten a hot and delicious pizza produced out of nowhere. He was convinced that in this special place everything was possible.

Over the past few decades, modern science has made rapid strides, *Manu Rishi* continued. But, you must understand that ancient *Vedic* science is thousands of years old and had made unimaginable progress in solving the mysteries of the entire universe. Quantum physics talks of dual nature of matter at sub atomic level. It talks of duality of wave as well as particle nature of matter. Instead of a deterministic model, modern science is slowly migrating towards a probabilistic model. Science is struggling to come up with one unified theory which explains the matter's behavior at macro and sub atomic level. On one hand, though explanations have been given on birth and death of stars, black holes and Quasars, a number of questions still remain unanswered. What is anti-matter and where is it? What actually happens at the event horizon? How does the birth of time take place... well; believe it or not... these questions have been scientifically researched by the great Indian spiritual masters thousands of years ago and detailed and elaborate explanations have been given for the various phenomena observed in nature. The ancient *Vedic* hymn *Hanuman (Hindu monkey God) Chalisa (hymn)* accurately calculates the distance between the Earth and the Sun and ancient spiritual texts *Ramayana* and *Mahabharata* give detailed and vivid accounts of aerial war fighting machines and other esoteric weapons almost equivalent to modern day nuclear and Laser weapons. However, all that has been stated in ancient texts is yet to be discovered by the modern world. The ancient monks and sages who had invented these path breaking technologies were aware of the repercussion of these technologies falling into the wrong and evil hands. That's the reason why most of the path breaking research which were being undertaken in *Takshshila* during the *Mauryan* reign concerned re-discovering ancient technology and innovations.

Wow! Exclaimed *John*. Those must be really exciting times. Yes they were, the old monk replied. Exciting and dangerous. Dangerous, *John* said with a look of surprise on his face. Yes, *Manu Rishi* replied. As I have told you, *Chandragupta*'s accession to the throne was not by peaceful means. He had to literally fight his way to the throne and in the process thousands of persons were killed and millions of destinies changed and rewritten. Both *Chandragupta* and *Chanakya* were acutely aware that they had enemies lurking around every corner of the world and that was one of the primary reasons for raising an army of spies. The *Mauryan* Empire was ruled with an iron hand. Strict discipline was enforced and people were sent to jail or killed on the merest of suspicion. Things were manageable till the time *Chandragupta* and *Chanakya* were alive. However, after *Chanakya*'s demise the *Mauryan* Empire lacked an able Prime Minister. It was slowly disintegrating. The void after *Chandragupta*'s death was made up after *Asoka* became the king, but the void of *Chanakya* could not be filled.

Kartik was a renowned scholar and contemporary of *Chanakya* at *Takshshila*. The debates between *Chanakya* and *Kartik* on varied subjects were a treat to witness. It was a known fact that if there was a scholar of political science who could challenge and match *Chanakya*, then it was only *Kartik*. However, with the passage of time and turn of events, *Kartik* developed a deep sense of hatred towards *Chanakya*. *Chanakya*'s rise as the Prime Minister and chief confidante of *Chandragupta* further fueled the jealousy and hatred which *Kartik* nurtured against *Chanakya*. He was smart and intelligent enough to guard his hatred and not share it with anyone, even with his own wife. Out worldly, *Kartik* was all praise for *Chanakya,* but in his mind, he was constantly scheming and looking for an opportunity to bring about the downfall of *Chanakya*.

When *Chanakya* was banished by King *Bindusara*, he realized that it was actually *Subandhu* who was manipulating the King. *Chanakya* realized that

Subandhu would go to any extent to kill him. He was not afraid of death. He firmly believed in the *Hindu* philosophy of rebirth and life after death. But, *Chanakya* did not want to die with the secret of the nine teams cremated along with his mortal remains. He needed to share the secret with a worthy successor who would utilize the enormous power of discoveries towards the good and benefit of mankind and continue to guard the secret.

Nishkam was the chief disciple of *Chanakya* and like him was a *bhramchari* (celibate) and had no worldly attachments. His only purpose in life was to serve his *guru* (Teacher/ Master). After being banished from the kingdom by King *Bindusara*, *Chanakya* called *Nishkam* to his private chamber and shared the entire secret of the nine teams with him. He swore *Nishkam* to absolute secrecy and instructed him to preserve the secret till such time he felt that a worthy successor of King *Bindusara* was present to look after and protect the teams. In case, any of the nine teams were to be in mortal danger, then only was *Nishkam* empowered to share the secret with the King and seek his assistance. *Chanakya* then met all the nine team leaders in the astral plane and told them to contact *Nishkam* after his death.

At *Takshshila*, though *Kartik* became suspicious of the activities being carried out in the prohibited region of the university, but his numerous attempts to gather information either resulted in stoic silence or in vague stories of supernatural beings and events. In spite of his best efforts, he was unable to find out the secret of the nine teams and never came to know when the teams left *Takshshila* and were relocated to different secret locations.

Kartik became a very frustrated and jealous person. In his mind, he started weaving stories about the ill treatment meted out to him by *Chanakya* and started attributing every misfortune to *Chanakya*. The distinction between reality and fantasy vanished and he started hallucinating about *Chanakya* and the various ways by which he will bring about his downfall. *Kartik* was desperately in the look out of a powerful king who could teach *Bindusara* a lesson and bring about the downfall of the *Mauryan Empire* and along with it the end of *Chanakya*. He found such a king in *Seleucus Necator*.

Of the nine secret teams which were relocated to secret destinations, *Kartik* came to have a whiff of research being carried out by one of the teams. In a fluke encounter in a liquor parlor near *Takshshila*, he came across a cattle grazer in an inebriated state who claimed to have witnessed a strange happening in the forest, when he had lost his way and had strayed deep inside it. The grazer's story was so strange that everyone present in the liquor parlor was mocking him and dismissing his tale as an outcome of fantasy born out of a drunken man's head. But *Kartik* thought that maybe there could be an iota of truth in the grazer's story. If true, *Kartik* knew that the discovery was capable of changing the entire history of mankind and was so valuable that kings would be ready to offer their kingdom in exchange of the secret. At last, *Kartik* knew that he had an offer for King *Seleucus Necator* which he simply would not refuse. The journey towards the downfall of *Chanakya* had begun.

So what was the secret that *Kartik* stumbled upon, *John* asked the old monk. Not so fast, dear friend, the monk replied. The cattle grazer in the liquor parlor said that he had seen a strange ceremony in which a group of men in white robes were chanting hymns while pouring a strange liquid over a lead idol which was slowly transforming from lead to gold. He said that in front of his eyes the entire idol had been converted to gold. Thereafter, the men had again poured some different liquid over the now gold idol while chanting some unknown hymn and reconverted it back to lead.

Oh! *John* exclaimed, isn't that alchemy. He knew that for centuries people have been talking about alchemy or transmutation of metals. In fact, old Indian folk lore is abundant with stories of temples receiving tons of gold as unknown donations during periods of drought and famine. From times immemorial, India has always been referred to as the golden bird with temples having huge quantities of gold stored in underground cellars. The huge quantity of gold available in India is quite surprising knowing that it has very less reservoir of gold deposits. There have been three separate schools of thought in the field of alchemy. The *Chinese* school based on the principles of *Tao*, the *Indian* school based on ancient philosophy of *Dharma* and the Western school centered around the *Mediterranean* and *Arabic* region based on secret sects and societies who believe in presence of a *Philosopher's Stone* having almost magical properties of turning base metals into noble metals. The search of the stone is also referred to as *Magnum Opus* or the Great Work.

Manu Rishi stood up and approached *John*. Here, I have a present for you; he said and pressed a gold coin in *John*'s hand. What, exclaimed *John*. He looked at the gold coin with awe. It was an irregular five punched coin. On one side was the symbol of *Asoka Pillar* with its famous lion face and on the reverse side was depicted a seven headed serpent raising its head in the middle of a sea and having a deity sitting in lotus position underneath it. A huge jewel was shown placed on top of the serpent's head. What the hell is that, *John* said. That, the monk replied, pointing at the jewel, is *Chintamani*… or the *Hindu* equivalent of *Philosopher's Stone*. The gold coin which I have given you belongs to the *Asoka* period.

What is a *Chintamani*, *John* asked, looking at the gold coin with deep intent. According to an old *Hindu* legend, in pre historic times, an iconic battle was fought between the celestial beings and demons, which was initially being dominated by the demons. In desperation, the celestial beings approached the creator for assistance who asked them to churn the oceans and from which will emerge an urn containing nectar which will make everyone who drinks it immortal. Since, there was no rope strong enough to churn the ocean, the celestial beings took the assistance of the King of serpents, the same seven headed serpent you see embossed on the coin to act as a rope and assist them in churning the oceans. Post the churning of the oceans, initially an urn containing deadly poison was produced which was swallowed by the *Hindu* God *Shiva*. Thereafter, a number of gifts with magical properties emerged from the ocean. One of them was *Chintamani* or the *Philosopher's Stone* which could transform base metals into noble metals and finally the urn containing the holy nectar capable of making beings immortal emerged, which was drunk by the celestial beings making them immortal and resulting in the victory of good over evil. What a story, *John* exclaimed. But do you seriously want me to believe this, he said laughing. The next thing that you will tell me is that the urn containing the immortality nectar also exists and is lying somewhere here in the mountains. The old monk became silent and went into deep meditation.

What I have done, thought *John*. I have annoyed the monk who was my only savior in this God forsaken place. You have not annoyed me, the old man said opening his eyes. Many cultures talk of a potion called elixir of life having qualities similar to the nectar revealed during the churning of the ocean. The universe is full of mysteries and unexplained phenomena. In fact, the *Hindus* believe that the whole creation is *Maya* or an elaborate illusion of the creator. We all are mere puppets enacting pre mediated roles, continuously believing that we are in control of our thoughts and actions while the Supreme Being smiles and amuses himself in this continuous game of life and death, creation and destruction.

Hey, hold it, *Jack* replied. Don't try to further confuse me. I have been patiently listening to you for a long time trying to find out the reason why I am here, but all I hear are a number of stories of ancient times and you talking in circles rather than coming straight to the point.

Be patient, dear friend, *Manu Rishi* replied. I have waited centuries to share the secret and take the burden off me and you are getting agitated in a few moments, he added. What secret, *John* asked. Do you think that I would believe your claim of having waited for centuries to share the secret with me? What nonsense, John said. I am not here to give proof of my words, the old man replied. The proof is in your conscience. If you believe from the core of your heart that what I am speaking is true, then there is no proof required. But if you suspect that I am making up stories to amuse you or confuse you then I will not stop you in your chosen life's journey and as promised will safely send you back to California, the old man replied. But, be patient, there is a lot of ground to be covered. *John* decided to let the monk finish his story before forming any opinion or taking any decision about his future course of action. Please continue, he said to the old monk.

Have you seen the *Asoka* pillar at *Qutub Minar* in Delhi, the old man asked? No, John replied. But what's so special about the pillar. Well, it's a seven meter tall iron pillar placed in the *Qutub* complex and has a unique property that it does not rust. It is an example of the advancements in the fields of metallurgy and science of that time, the monk said. Well, the iron pillar is no proof of the existence of *Chintamani*, *John* said. For the first time *John* saw the old monk slightly agitated. If I told you that the alchemists of that time had deliberately altered the chemical properties of iron to make it rust free, will you still not believe me, the monk replied with a hint of anger in his tone.

I believe you all along, *John* replied. Had I not believed in you then I would not have undertaken this great and hazardous journey or be sitting right across you at this moment, he added. What you are telling me is incredible and frankly difficult to believe. But, you yourself are an incredible man. Of what little I have seen of you or interacted with you, I realize that you are no ordinary being and are on a mission which definitely involves me. I have full faith in you but frankly am too tired right now and unable to concentrate. I need to sleep. The events of the day have been too much for me; John said tiredly trying hard to hide his yawn.

Oh! I am so sorry, the monk replied. I have been waiting for you for such a long time that I am in a hurry to tell you everything in one go, especially with the events which are happening all around. What events, *John* asked. I will tell you everything, the monk replied. But first you lie down and go off to sleep. The words had barely left the old monk's lips and *John* fell off into a deep slumber.

Wake up *John*, wake up... It's daybreak and we have a long journey to undertake. The words literally jolted *John* out of his slumber. He was in the same cave but somehow, the temperature seemed to be regulated, he was not at all feeling cold and was fully refreshed and energized. The old monk was sitting cross legged in his usual position and was looking at him with a steady gaze as if his body was here but the soul was travelling in a distant far off land.

Wow! I feel relaxed and refreshed, said *John* after getting up. I feel no hunger or thirst and a strange sensation of peace is enveloping me, he said. Where are we going, he asked the monk. You ask too many questions, *Manu Rishi* replied. I will answer all your questions when the time is ripe. But at least tell me about the nine secret teams, *John* asked. You have only told me about the alchemists, what about the others, he asked getting inquisitive and impatient at the same time.

The first team researched on propaganda and psychological warfare, *Manu Rishi* replied. A great deal of findings was put to practice by *Chanakya* during the Mauryan reign under *Chandragupta Maurya*. In fact, a major portion of his treatise *Arthashastra* is devoted to this subject. Have you ever wondered how a small army under a commoner was able to overthrow the *Nanda* Empire in such a short span of time? *Chanakya* had changed the rules of the game. He did not fight in the manner in which the *Nanda* Empire was used to fighting or wanted him to fight. Instead, he forced them to fight according to his own rules when he was strong and they weak. Propaganda and psychological warfare were the force multipliers in his arsenal which he used very effectively to demoralize and spread fear and confusion in the enemy's ranks. In fact, a great deal of interest in *Chanakya*'s life and philosophy of war fighting was shown by the Germans during Hitler's time who believed that they were the true *Aryan* race and actual descendants of the *Indo Gangetic* civilization.

The second team researched into physiology. We have not been able to discover the true potential of our bodies, the monk continued. Like a universe outside, there is a universe inside our bodies and we have only a fraction of knowledge about this inner universe. The second team had some very fine breakthroughs. They were able to regulate the body temperature to adapt to the outside temperature so that the body became warm when the outside temperature was cold and cool when the outside temperature was hot. They were able to regulate the heart beat and breathing process in order to place the body through a regulated hibernation process in order to escape harsh climatic conditions without food and water. Research on longevity was carried out with remarkable results. It is said that certain death holds of ancient martial art forms like *Judo* and *Ju Jitsu* have been acquired by Buddhist monks from the second team to protect the monasteries from invading tribes of robbers and dacoits.

The third team researched on microbiology. Since ancient times, the water of *Ganga* has been believed to have sacred and almost magical properties. People suffering from a host of ailments including leprosy have shown miraculous cure after taking a bath in the holy river or drinking its water. Do you know that the water of the river has this unique property that it does not leave an odor or putrefy even if it is bottled for years together and also of self-cleansing and self-healing. Recent scientific studies of the rivers water have proved that the water possesses bactericidal properties or the ability to kill bacteria which has been attributed to the extraordinary presence of *bacteriophage* in the water. What is *bacteriophage, John* asked. Phages are highly strain specific viruses with a unique property of targeting specific bacteria's. Thus, phages are the ultimate drug against disease because unlike antibiotics, the phages target only the specific disease causing bacteria. People with cholera have been known to have been cured of their disease by just drinking the water from *Ganga*. Unbelievable, *John* said. Yes, the monk replied and it is believed that the waters of *Ganga* are mixed with potent mixtures created by the third secret team at its source which gives the river such extraordinary properties.

The fourth secret team researched in communications including non-verbal and those with extra-terrestrial beings. You must have realized that sometimes you can communicate better without words. We regularly communicate with our pets and other animals. In fact, communication is an intrinsic quality of all living and non-living things in this universe. Not only are living beings communicating with each other but elements of nature and the entire creation are in continuous state of communication, *Manu Rishi* said.

The fifth team researched on cosmology and space time travel to distant planets and universe by transiting through various space time fabrics, the monk continued. What do you mean by various space time fabrics, *John* asked. Well, the old monk replied, the concept of time as we know it, is quite peculiar. Say, if I ask you whether we are going forward or backward in time, then you will find it difficult to explain. We associate direction of time with entropy, which is a measure of orderliness in any object. When time travels in the forward direction, then the associated entropy of an object changes from a state of orderliness to disorderliness. A rock left alone over a period of time will crumble and disintegrate. Recent breakthrough in science have shown that time as a dimension is not linear but slightly warped around a particular space to create the notion of one world or universe; however there are many such universes and worlds having their own space time matrices. Research into various space time matrices to enable inter dimensional travel was being carried out by the fifth team.

The sixth team researched on gravity, especially with respect to technology for building super-fast aircrafts. What, *John* asked in astonishment. Are you trying to tell me that people in ancient times were aware of aircrafts and air travel. Of course, the monk replied. The ancient spiritual texts *Ramayana* and *Mahabharata* both talk of aerial vehicles and space ships. But, the sixth's team research went even further. The team was harnessing the potential of gravity by selectively increasing and decreasing it in order to make space ships capable of carrying enormous load and still travel at fast speeds, more so for inter planetary travel. Amazing, *John* said.

The seventh team researched on light. Just like in today's era we have been able to concentrate the light waves into synchrony and create lasers, similarly the seventh team could built light based weapons which were capable of causing more death and destruction than the modern day nuclear weapons. But, the team was strictly given a mandate not to develop weapons but use its research to achieve breakthrough which would help in the peaceful coexistence of the entire world.

The eighth team studied sociology or the rules governing rise and fall of societies and civilizations. The team could artificially trigger the rise or decline of various societies or nation states. As told earlier, the ninth team devoted its research on alchemy. The old monk suddenly became silent and again went into his meditative mode leaving John quiet, astonished and excited. What has destiny in store for me, he thought. But, whatever it is, I am sure that it would be a hell of a ride.

John waited patiently for the old monk to come out of his state. How much time have I spent in this cave, he wondered. The old monk stirred and laughed. Time is notional, he said. What do you mean by notional, *John* asked. Well as I have already explained to you that the concept of time has been associated with entropy. It is also associated with the speed of light. That is why the radiations of distant stars which we are receiving at the present moment have originated years back in time and has given rise to an astronomical unit called light year. Einstein has proved that by travelling faster than light you can go back and forth in time. I am aware of that, but there is no matter in this universe which can travel faster than the speed of light, *John* replied getting slightly irritated. Is it so, the monk asked? Absolutely, *John* replied. But what about thoughts, *Manu Rishi* said. Don't you visualize moments in your mind of past and future all the time. So in effect, your thoughts obey Einstein's rationale and hence are able to travel in past and future all the time. But my thoughts are just games of my semi-conscious mind and nothing else, *John* replied. Let us imagine for a moment that you are in a state of mind where no thoughts are entering your mind. The mind is completely blank yet fully aware of the present. I have never experienced such a state, *John* replied. Very few have, the old monk said slowly.

But if you attain that state and remain in that state then time actually stops, there is no entropy and you remain as it is while the people and universe around you keeps on decaying and changing. You become time independent. The power to stop time is in your hands. The monk then became silent.

Unbelievable, *John* said. Where do I fit inside all this? After *Chanakya*'s death, *Nishkam* was the only person who knew about the secret of the nine teams. It was *Chanakya*'s directions that the secret of the nine teams should always be shared by two persons so that in case of an unexpected demise of one, the other person would be able to keep the secret alive as well as assist the teams in case of any requirement. After *Chanakya*'s death, the secret of the teams was passed on to *Asoka* by *Nishkam* after the battle of *Kalinga* when *Asoka* had embraced *Buddhism*. This tradition of sharing the secret among two persons has continued since then. So you mean to say that you are one of the holders of the secret, *John* asked in awe. The old monk slowly nodded his head. And now you my friend are the other, he slowly replied. The words sent an electric current through *John*'s entire being. A deep surge of strong emotions swept through his body. Not only was he experiencing extreme excitement and thrill but was filled with shock, disbelief and utmost fear. He knew in his heart that very few of the persons who possessed such a powerful secret could lead a normal and carefree life and would have died a natural death surrounded by their near and dear ones during their final moments.

4

The news that he was one of the only two persons alive in the world who knew the secret of the nine teams had sent *John* into a shock. It was quite a while after which he regained his composure and asked, why me? What have I done to know the secret? The old monk looked intently at *John* and continued. As I have told earlier, *Karthik* had got a whiff of the secret team and had joined the court of *Selucid Necator* in order to match *Chanakya*'s name and fame. With a burning desire to teach a lesson to *Chanakya*, he shared the secret of the alchemy team with *Selucid Necator*. The king immediately launched his entire network of spies to hunt down the team. At that particular moment, the team was on its way to its secret destination in the *Himalayas*.

The news of a group of persons moving from *Takshshila* to *Himalayas* reached *Selucid Necator*. He immediately launched his army to hunt down the team and bring the leader to him. *Chanakya*, also through his network of spies came to know of the plans of *Selucid Necator* and immediately warned all teams to be careful and avoid contact with villagers and strangers. The battle between the *Selucid Necator*'s army and the alchemy team took place at *Rupkund* lake at the base of *Trishul*

Mastiff. Today also hundreds of skeletons can be seen at the base of the river. In spite of being a small group with no conventional weapons, the alchemy team was able to decimate a major portion of *Selucid Necator*'s army using the powerful light concentration weapons given to them as a last resort, for their protection. The team also suffered losses including death of several women and children. But, the biggest loss was the compromise of the secret and confirmation of the existence of the alchemy team as well as the existence of a powerful light emitting weapon. Though, the team was able to reach its destination uninterrupted after the battle of *Rupkund*, but the global search for the secret teams had started. It marked the beginning of a cat and mouse game which continues to be played till today. The old monk again went into deep meditation as if giving time to *John* to absorb and be mentally prepared for the next revelation.

So you mean to say that the nine secret teams still exist today and that there are people who are trying to get their secret at any cost. Just observe the happenings around the world and you would realize the truth in my words, the old monk continued. There are innumerable reports of sighting of strange aerial vehicles, Stonehenge, crop patterns, ancient Mayan civilization, African voodoo, miracles of holy saints, the talking heads of *Pope Sylvester II*, lost city of *Dwaraka*, reports of *sadhus* possessing extraordinary powers... the list is endless.

But you have still not answered my one basic question, asked *John*. Why me and what am I doing here. The old man closed his eyes and became silent. Before I reveal anything further I want a commitment from you, the old monk slowly said. What commitment, *John* asked. I want a commitment that you will never disclose the secrets of the nine teams to anyone at any cost except to my successor in case of my death, whom you will choose. The knowledge which I will impart to you will give you enormous powers and would transform your life in more than one ways. You have to promise me that you will never demonstrate the powers in public and will only use them as a last resort to save yourself or the lives of innocent beings. From now on you will have to lead the life of a celibate *sadhu* and shun human company. You will live alone in seclusion for the rest of your life. You will not possess any material comforts and live with the single pointed aim of protecting the teams at all cost, including your own life. You have to break loose all ties with friends and families and become free of any kind of attachment. Only once you agree to these terms, can we further progress the conversation. Once the commitment has been given, there would be no going back. For all purposes you will die and a new person would be born, free and fearless.

John became still. The old monk's words echoed in his ears. You have to live a life of a celibate *sadhu* and shun human company for the rest of your life. What a great price to pay to know a secret which might or might not even exist. His whole life flashed past him. The love and affection of his parents and grandparents, the luxurious and comfortable life in California, the cool time spent with friends. But, somehow in his heart *John* knew that he would never be able to live again if he walked out from the cave without listening to the monk. He was standing on the edge of a mighty cliff confused and scared. Then *John* took the giant leap of faith from the edge, ready to fly and explore the vast and unchartered territory. I promise, he said. *John* suddenly felt liberated of all earthly shackles. A great weight as if had suddenly lifted off his chest. He knew that the decision which he had just taken would exact a very heavy price from him, but he was ready because his whole existence was there just to be a part of the secret society and serve them. He was sure of his aim in this life.

The old monk smiled. I knew that you would say yes, he said. The service of the secret society has been your single purpose for many lives. As the *Geeta* (*Hindu* religious text) says, like we discard old and worn out clothes and wear fresh ones, similarly the human soul continuously discards bodies and enters new ones. The soul never dies, only the external appearances keep on changing. The attachment to external elements like wealth, material possessions, friends and family is transitory. By letting go, you become free. Free from fear and death, because the task which you have accepted requires you to be fearless from each cell of your being. There is no scope of even a single unwarranted thought entering your mind. We have a lot of ground to cover and time is less. The forces of evil are gathering in strength as we speak and for the first time, the secret society is facing unprecedented danger from a number of quarters. My time is limited. I am ready to face the ultimate challenge in this birth and am satisfied that I have chosen a worthy guardian of the society. There was a sense of urgency and purpose in the monk's words. *John* knew that danger was lurking around the corner and he needed to be fully prepared to face it, if he was to emerge victorious and save the secret society.

The old monk suddenly became silent. I feel the presence of our enemies nearby. We need to leave this cave now, he said. A chill ran down *John*'s spine. What enemies, he said and how have you sensed them. There will be enough time to provide explanations to you afterwards, but we need to move out now. Saying this, the old monk quickly extinguished the earthen lamp, suddenly plunging the entire cave in pitch black darkness and holding *John*'s hand started moving into the recesses of the cave. The entrance to the cave is towards the other side, *John* said. I know, the monk replied and moved with a sure footedness as if he did not require eyes to make his way inside the bowels of the Earth.

The cave started becoming narrow as *John* and the monk started moving towards its depth. The level of oxygen was also reducing which coupled with the stale air made *John* nauseous and suffocating. Wait, he said. Why are we running? I don't hear or see any one. Moreover, I am feeling dizzy and suffocating. There is pitch black darkness and I am experiencing nervousness and fear like I have never felt before. The old monk slowed down a bit. We have to keep moving, he said. Unlike yours, my senses are extremely sharp and fully developed. I can sense the presence of evil men in the surroundings and hear their footsteps as they search the mountains looking for us. We are running from them not because I am afraid of facing them, but this is not the opportune moment to face them. We will fight and defeat them, at the right time and at the right place, according to our terms. You are not ready yet. They don't know about you and I want them to think that I am now the only guardian left to defend the society.

The old monk stopped suddenly. They had reached the end of the cave. *John* could feel the walls of the cave narrowing and converging in the middle. There is no escape route, he thought. Don't be impatient, the old monk replied. He knelt down and started removing the rubble from the floor of the cave. Soon enough a narrow opening became visible through which only a single person could barely squeeze in. You go in first, the monk nudged *John*. Slowly, *John* got down to his knees and started squeezing himself through the narrow opening. Though, he could not see anything but he could feel that the walls of the chamber were smooth, as if this passage was used earlier too. He was all alone. The monk had left his hand when he had asked him to enter the small opening. *John* started crawling forward. Suddenly, he heard the noise of rocks crumbling and falling and a wave of dust and debris started filling the narrow chamber. The passage was so narrow that *John* could not turn back and moreover he was getting suffocated with lack of oxygen and dust entering his mouth and nostrils. He wanted to scream but words failed to come out of his mouth. *John* felt a wave of pure unadulterated fear overpower him. He lost his bearing and panicked, totally incapable of thinking straight. I am about to die and no one will ever come to know of it, he thought. The old man was gone, lost behind the thick veil of dust and rock. *John* was all alone and slowly losing his consciousness. The walls of the cave were slowly closing up on him.

Don't give up, a voice floated into his subconscious. *John* slowly gathered his wits around himself and started crawling forward. I have to keep moving, he said to himself. I will either find a way or make one. With renewed energy he started crawling forward. *John*, don't look back, the monk's voice floated in his head. Where are you, *John* shouted. Don't bother about me, just keep going. Go to *Haridwar*, somebody would be waiting for you there. The narrow cavity was suddenly opening up. In the far distance, *John* could see a thin stream of light coming through a small opening. I am almost there, he said to himself. I need to get out and rush back to save the monk. After a while, *John* pushed his way out from the opening and started breathing the fresh and chilly air of the mountain side. Not a soul was in sight and a vast stretch of open plateau was spread out in front of him. Behind him, the mountain range extended till as far as his eyes could see. The only way left to go was forward into unknown and unchartered territory leaving *Manu Rishi* behind all alone to fight the evil forces. With a heavy heart *John* decided to move on. He knew that the monk was highly accomplished and would contact him whenever he wanted. His aim now was to somehow reach *Haridwar* (Abode of God), where the next part of his journey was waiting to begin.

Haridwar

According to *Hindus*, *Haridwar* is one of the seven holiest places in India. As the story goes, after *Samudra Manthan* or the celestial churning of the oceans, the elixir of life or *Amrit* was being carried by *Garud* the powerful celestial bird of God *Bhrama* (the creator) in a pitcher when four drops of it were spilled at *Haridwar*, *Nasik*, *Ujjain* and *Prayag* or modern day *Allahabad*. This is the reason that the *Kumbh Mela*, the largest congregation of mankind in the entire world, is celebrated every three years in rotation at these places resulting in a twelve year cycle of the mega event at each place. The place where the *Amrit* fell at *Haridwar* is referred to as *Bhram Kund* and the *ghat* (bank) along the river called *Har Ki Pauri* (steps of God). The evening prayers at *Har Ki Pauri* draw a large number of devotees and visitors to the banks of *Ganga*. Amidst the flowing waters of the river, thousands of priests chant hymns in glory of the river goddess and light floating lamps creating an enchanting and surreal atmosphere.

John stood at *Har Ki Pauri* watching the evening prayers. With great difficulty he had managed to reach *Haridwar* and had taken shelter in one of the numerous *ashrams* (religious resting place) doting the town's landscape. The gold coin in his pocket was a silent reminder that the meeting with the monk was real and not a figment of his imagination. He had reached *Haridwar*, but was clueless now. *John* sensed a deep transformation taking place inside him after his meeting with the monk and his escape from Tibet under difficult and tiring circumstances. He was talking less and living in the present with no worries about the future. There was this great feeling of self-confidence that no matter what, he would be able to face the challenges that would confront him. The act of living in the present with no worries about the future was liberating. Like a free bird, which has no idea where her next morsel of food would come from but lived each moment brimming with joy and happiness singing her song; deep down *John* was experiencing a sense of happiness and emotional satisfaction in a way that he had never experienced before. His senses were becoming keener, his breathing relaxed, his walk slow and a thin smile on his lips gave a glimpse of his inside world to the outer world.

Welcome my friend, the words startled *John* who was deeply engrossed in watching the *aarti* (prayer) at the banks of *Ganga*. He turned around to see a *sadhu* addressing him. The man looked familiar. Oh my God, he is the same *sadhu* who had laughed at me at *Allahabad* when I had my first experience at seventeen, *John* exclaimed. So, how did your meeting with *Manu Rishi* go, the *sadhu* asked. *John* was taken aback. How on earth does this person know that I had met *Manu Rishi*, he wondered. The entire meeting was inside a cave in a secluded place having no habitation for miles around. Don't think too much, the *sadhu* replied. Saying this, he started moving with rapid strides along the *ghats* and slowly disappeared in the sea of humanity thronging the *ghats* at this time of the evening. *John* had practically no time to react. Wait, he said and started taking long strides trying to catch up with the *sadhu* as he swiftly went into one of the numerous small by lanes adjoining the *ghats* and disappeared from sight.

John broke into a jog, trying to catch up with the *sadhu*. He did not want to lose sight of him for even a moment. He looked around and suddenly caught sight of the *sadhu* walking rapidly away from the hustle and bustle of the main town. He heaved a sigh of relief and again started following the *sadhu*. After leaving the town, the *sadhu* suddenly entered a cremation ground where a number of dead bodies were being cremated. Each pyre had a small group of the deceased person's relatives huddled around the burning pyre with a priest chanting sacred hymns and pouring large quantities of *ghee* (clarified butter) onto the pyre. The method of performing last rites according to *Hindu* customs has remained unchanged for the past thousands of years. *Chandi Ghat*, the board outside the cremation ground read. It was getting dark and the only light illuminating the entire place were the burning pyres at various places around the entire ground. In spite of the dark surroundings, the cremation ground was not at all frightening. In fact, the quiet and silence was a welcome change from the maddening crowd and by lanes of the congested town. The *sadhu* was slowly moving towards the extremities of the cremation ground where a thatched hut was standing. He entered the hut which had no door and slowly looked at *John* as if asking him to come inside. John was taken aback. The person he was following was not the *sadhu* he had met at *Har Ki Pauri*. He had been fooled by the long unkempt matted hair and the saffron robes, which were commonly worn by all the *sadhus*. He was in a fix. Should he go back and search for the lost *sadhu* or enter the hut. After a while, *John* entered the hut.

A strange sight greeted *John* as soon as he entered the hut. A bare chested *sadhu* with long matted hair and beard was sitting around a small fire and drinking liquor from a human skull which had vermillion smeared around it. The fire was casting strange shadow of the *sadhu* with the skull and gave the whole place an eerie look.

The *sadhu* looked up and smiled. It was one of the most innocent smiles that *John* had ever seen. The smile of a newly born child. The smile of a person who has nothing to hide, nothing to ask, but only to give. The whole atmosphere of the hut suddenly changed from a dark and eerie place to a warm and welcoming one. The simple gesture of the *sadhu* had literally transformed the entire surroundings. Greetings my son, the *sadhu* spoke in *John*'s mind. I am *Rishi Kripal* and this is my *chela* or disciple *Kalyan*. We have been sent by *Manu* to assist you in your journey.

John was spellbound. But the last I saw of *Manu Rishi* was him all alone in a cave in Tibet fighting with evil forces, he said. Then, how is it possible that he has contacted you and asked you to help me, *John* added. The world is full of mysteries, the *sadhu* replied. I met *Manu* during a recent astral journey where he asked me to assist you in your fight against evil forces. What evil forces, *John* asked. I don't know, the *sadhu* replied. But I do know that evil like goodness is a part and parcel of this creation. Like every action has an equal and opposite reaction, similarly good and evil exist side by side. Evil is not limited to humans alone. Evil is in the spirit and the spirit can reside anywhere, in any form, human or otherwise, animate or inanimate, in this world or another.

John was stunned. He did not know whether to trust the *sadhu* or not. But one thing was sure, the *sadhu* was aware of his meeting with *Manu Rishi* and was hiding more than revealing, he said to himself. Why you guys always talk in circles, *John* asked. The *sadhu* started laughing. John was taken aback as he really could not understand the joke. The *sadhu* suddenly became silent. We do not talk in circles, he said. It is just that we are more aware than you. Now, it was *John*'s time to smile. This semi naked man in a thatched hut in the midst of a cremation ground in *Haridwar* was more aware than a person who lived in California and had roamed around half of the world.

Rishi Kripal smiled and said, *Manu* was fighting evil at different levels. The easiest level to fight is at the physical level where we can see evil and feel it. But evil does not exist only at the physical level; it resides at different levels, even within us. The creation is multi-dimensional. By saying that I am more aware than you, I meant to convey that while you might have roamed around this world, maybe more than me, but I have been to and have knowledge of many such different worlds, which you not only don't know but cannot simply imagine. Therefore, rightly so I am more aware than you. The *sadhu* became silent. Where is *Manu Rishi*? John asked. That I cannot reveal, *Rishi Kripal* replied. But, he has asked me to assist you in your journey, which is dangerous and full of challenges. You can consider him dead for all practical purposes, the *sadhu* added.

Tears welled up in *John*'s eyes. Though his association with *Manu Rishi* was very short in terms of time but it had had a profound impact on him at various levels. He had made a promise to him and now the time had come to fulfill that promise. So what next, *John* asked *Rishi Kripal*. I can only impart my inner knowledge to you if you become my *chela* and that involves complete and total surrender to me. You will not question me and simply obey whatever I tell you. The knowledge which I would impart is secret. You cannot share it with anyone. Are you ready to become my *chela*? John nodded in affirmative. Good, the *sadhu* said. First, you have to die and have a new birth. What, *John* exclaimed.

5

Rishi Kripal was walking briskly along the banks of *Ganga* with *John* trying his level best to catch up with him. The *sadhu* was holding an earthen pot which was filled with the ash from a smoldering pyre at *Chandi Shamshan Ghat* (cremation ground). He quickly entered one of the numerous by lanes along the *ghat* and stood in front of an old two storied ramshackled building. Is *Pandit Ramchandra Sahay* at home he bellowed? Who is it, a hoarse voice asked from within. Tell the *Pandit, Rishi Kripal* is here. The door was suddenly opened by an old man dressed in sparkling white *dhoti* and *kurta*. In spite of his age, the *pandit* stood ram rod straight with a regal bearing and bright red vermillion applied in three horizontal lines across his forehead. Welcome my friend, he said and embraced the *sadhu*. What brings you to my humble abode?

I want you to immerse the holy ashes of an acquaintance in the *Ganga* and make an entry in his ancestral ledger. Since times immemorial, the *pandits* of *Haridwar* are maintaining the genealogical trees of *Hindu* families based on their *caste* and *gotras*. It is the sacred duty of each *Hindu* to immerse the ashes of his kith and kin at *Haridwar* and thereafter meet the family priest and enter the birth, marriage and death details in the family ledgers maintained by the priest. Thus, the entire lineage of a family can be traced back many centuries. John was aware of this custom as he had seen his grandfather too maintain a ledger of his family tree. Who is the acquaintance, the *pandit* asked. The name is *Gyanendra* of *Kashyap gotra* and grandson of *Pandit Ram Murat*, the sadhu said. *John* was taken aback. His *Hindu* name was *Gyanendra* and his grandfather's name was *Pandit Ram Murat*. In effect, the *sadhu* was effectively performing his last rites and entering his name in the ultimate list of dead *Hindus*.

After entering *John*'s name in *Pandit Ramchandra Sahay*'s ledger, *Rishi Kripal* again started walking briskly towards the *ghats* of holy *Ganga*. Remove all your clothes, the *sadhu* spoke to *John*. *John* was taken aback but did as he was ordered as he had accepted *Rishi Kripal* as his guru and was now duty bound to obey all his commands. When *John* was stark naked and standing fully uncovered in the sea of humanity, he suddenly felt liberated. Initially, he had a deep sense of fear and shame in getting naked in front of strangers, a habit which he had inherited from his parents. But now, when he was naked and standing in the middle of the crowd, *John* realized that his fears and sense of shame were unfounded. Nobody was making fun of him or ridiculing him. In fact, people were just not bothered. He realized that a larger part of his life had been wasted due to unfound fears and shame. These two emotions were so powerful that they were literally holding him back. By a single command, *Rishi Kripal* had liberated him.

Go and take a dip in the holy river and come back, *Rishi Kripal* said gently. *John* slowly walked down the steps of the *ghat* and reached the edge where the fast moving river current was swirling and making small eddies in the water. The water is really cold, were the first thoughts that struck *John* as he took his first baby steps towards the mighty river. When he was waist deep, he followed the *Hindu* ritual of taking a dip in the holy river. With palms joined together in a *Namaste,* he fully immersed himself in the river and chanted loudly "*Ganga Maiya ki Jai* (Hail Mother Ganga)". *Ganga Maiya Ki Jai,* he shouted again and immersed himself for the second time inside the river. The water was all around him and suddenly everything became silent. The continuous chatter in his mind stopped. There was no sound, no words and no thoughts. There was nothing. *John* had experienced nothing like this before. The silence created a Tsunami of peace and tranquility that swept through every cell of his being. The feeling was so intense that *John* could not handle it and emerged out of the water gasping for air. The silence had been shattered. All around him there was noise and commotion.

John again took a dip inside the water, but the feeling never returned. He kept on trying, but in vain. Exhausted, *John* realized that there was something more than the mechanical actions of chanting and immersing oneself in the river. Mother *Ganga* was sending him a message but what, he did not know.

John slowly got out of the river onto the bank where his *guru* was standing. Come, he said, let's take a haircut. *John*, still naked was taken to one of the numerous barbers lining the *ghats* and had his head tonsured. Thereafter, he was given a saffron robe to wear along with wooden slippers called *khadau* and a small brass pot called *kamandal*. With these material possessions, *John* and his *guru* started walking away from the holy river and *Haridwar*.

Rishi Kripal and *John* boarded a bus which took them to *Badrinath* after crossing *Joshimath*. The landscape had changed from plains of *Haridwar* to foothills of *Rishikesh* to mountains of *Joshimath* and *Badrinath*. Established by *Adi* (ancient) *Shankracharya* in eighth century BC, the *Badrinath* temple is one of the *Char* (Four) *Dhams* (Important Religious Site) of the *Hindus* and is dedicated to *Lord Vishnu*. It lies on the banks of the mighty *Alaknanda* River and is supposed to be guarded by two mountains *Nar* (man) and *Narayan* (God) with the majestic peak of *Neelkanth* in the background. After praying at the temple, *Rishi Kripal* started walking towards the *Neelkanth* peak with *John* in tow. The town and civilization were slowly left behind and the concrete jungle was giving way to greenery and Mother Nature. There was not a soul in sight.

It was getting dark. The jungle was closing in on them but the *sadhu* was in no mood to stop. We need to stop as it is getting dark, *John* said gathering courage. The *sadhu* laughed out loudly. What dark, he said. The modern world has blunted your senses. You have a lot to unlearn. After walking for an hour, the duo stopped in the middle of a clearing. It was totally dark now and *John* could hardly see a thing. He was just trying his level best to catch up with the *sadhu* who was walking with such confidence as if he was taking a stroll around his backyard. *John* found a thick boulder and slumped down on it. His whole body ached. His feet had blisters from the wooden slippers, his face and skin were scratched at a number of places by the numerous bushes and shrubs and he was shivering from the chill which was setting in. *John* felt miserable and dejected. The *sadhu* on the other hand was busy collecting branches, twigs and heather and erecting a makeshift shelter for the two of them. *John* felt guilty. He wanted to help but his body would just not relent to move even an inch. To add to the woes, his stomach was growling. They had not eaten a morsel since they had left *Haridwar*.

What do we eat, *John* asked the *sadhu*. The creator has catered for the needs of each and every one of his creations, the *sadhu* replied. First, we need to create a shelter for the night before you become the food of a hungry creation, the *sadhu* said laughing. *John* was getting irritated. Here we are in the middle of nowhere, with no light, food, clothes and shelter and the *sadhu* is busy making merry as if he was in an English pub having a drink and watching football with his buddies. The *sadhu* laughed again. I don't understand you, he said. Your irritation, fright and sadness are not going to take us anywhere. It will neither provide us with light, shelter, food or clothes. In fact, it will spiral out of control making you more irritated, sad and frightened which would ultimately result in you waiting for the moment when a God's creation comes, eats you and ends your misery. On the other hand, if you have confidence in your abilities and faith in the creator, then there is absolutely no need to worry and feel depressed. There is food, clothes, light and shelter already waiting for us. We just need to sense the silent message of the creator, find the necessities and carry on with life. Only those, who don't have faith in themselves or in the creator, worry and despair.

Soon, *Rishi Kripal* had created a small clearing, made a small thatched shelter and with the collected dry twigs and leaves had a small fire burning which he had ignited by rubbing two rocks; the way our ancestors created fire a long time ago. He vanished into the woods and returned with some fruits and leaves. Here, apply these leaves to your skin. It will relieve the itching as well as prevent the mosquitoes and other insects from biting you. Afterwards, eat this fruit. It is sweet and juicy and will take care of your fluid as well as nutritional requirements, the *sadhu* said. After applying the leaves and eating the delicious fruit, *John* felt relaxed and satiated. Now go off to sleep, the *sadhu* instructed. We will start our lessons at day break tomorrow. Barely had the words left *Rishi Kripal*'s mouth that *John* had slumped down inside the shelter, deep asleep.

A shrill cry suddenly woke up *John* from his sleep. What is this, he shouted. It was still dark and the burning embers of the fire built by *Rishi Kripal* were casting strange shadows on the ground. The *sadhu* was nowhere to be seen and the jungle seemed to be awake from all sort of noises. *Rishi Kripal*, *John* shouted in panic. The surroundings were again shattered by the shrill cry, sending a sharp chill down *John*'s spine. He was unable to make out whether the cry was of a human or an animal's. It seemed to be sort of a wail or a primordial guttural made due to anger or fear. *John* suddenly saw the *sadhu* emerge from the thick foliage. What was that sound, *John* asked? Nothing, the *sadhu* replied. Just a jungle beast hunting its prey. It is going to be daybreak soon and we need to get going, he said. A few moments later, *John* and *Rishi Kripal* left the clearing and started moving towards the mountains. Somehow, *John* was not convinced with the *sadhu*'s answer, but having made him his *guru*, he was duty bound to trust him absolutely, even with his own life.

The climb was getting steep. Adding to John's woes were the sores from the wooden sandals. *Rishi Kripal* seems to be so fit, *John* said to himself. I need to pay more attention to my weight as well as fitness levels. Can we rest for a while; *John* asked *Rishi Kripal* panting and tired from exhaustion. The climb was taking its toll on *John* and he was finding it difficult to keep pace with *Rishi Kripal*. OK, the *sadhu* said, but for a little while only. We need to reach our destination before night fall. After resting for a while, the duo resumed their journey. The beauty of the surroundings was breath taking. The slopes were lined with a variety of wild flowers and tall pine trees rose high in the sky. Deep below, a small rivulet flowed and there was not a man or man-made object in sight. The sounds of their footsteps were occasionally broken by the sweet melodious chirp of a variety of birds. It is so peaceful out here, *John* thought.

The *sadhu* suddenly stopped in front of a huge boulder. What he is doing, *John* thought? Come, *Rishi Kripal* said and started moving towards the edge of the boulder that was facing the steep drop of the mountain. *John* gingerly followed the *sadhu*. As he reached the edge of the boulder, he saw that the base of it was hidden by thick shrubs and branches and there was a small path leading down beneath the boulder. In fact, the boulder was so precariously placed along the mountain side that any person would definitely avoid it to prevent himself from slipping and falling into the deep valley. *John* followed the *sadhu* on the small path which had disappeared around the bend and beneath the boulder. What if the boulder dislodges and falls on my head, *John* thought as he moved quickly along the path to catch up with *Rishi Kripal*. As he turned the bend, *John* was completely taken aback. This was definitely a man-made path that was such elegantly made that it was completely hidden from sight from all sides. The portion towards the mountain side was concealed by numerous shrubs and branches so that a person even with a powerful binocular would find it impossible to detect it. The secret path was leading to a cave inside the mountain.

John entered the cave which had surprisingly opened up to reveal a large interior. Fresh air and light were streaming through the shrubs and branches covering the entrance. In one corner of the cave was a raised platform with a deerskin and an earthen lamp.

The cave was almost similar to the one of *Manu Rishi*. *Rishi Kripal* sat down on the deer skin and addressed *John*. This cave is going to be your home and school for the next few months. I will teach you all that I know and prepare you to take on the evil forces. We will begin our lessons, first thing in the morning. You will cook, clean and guard when you are not learning. You are physically weak and your will power and self-confidence low. There is too much arrogance and limited desire to learn. Saying this, the *sadhu* closed his eyes and went into deep meditation leaving *John* to figure out the next course of action.

John decided to explore his surroundings while the *sadhu* was doing his meditation. The cave was in all respects a more secure and better place to stay as compared to the previous day's shelter. He found the cave to be quite big for the two of them and decided to construct a small hearth towards the back for cooking meals. *John* thereafter ventured out and followed the narrow path which was leading away from the cave and towards a bend on the mountain side. A few yards away, a small rivulet fell from the mountain top, provisioning all the fresh and clear water he would ever require. *John* splashed the cool water on his face and drank some from the cusp of his hands. The water was very refreshing and soothing. He moved ahead and found a number of different varieties of shrubs and plants. Some of them were bearing exotic fruits while others were emanating aromatic scent from their flowers. I have never seen such beautiful and different varieties of plants in my life, *John* said to himself. And there is a lot more which you would be seeing for the first time in your life, the *sadhu*'s voice echoed from behind him. *John* turned around to see *Rishi Kripal* standing in front of him with a soft smile on his face. You should not venture out so far without informing me, he said. *John* nodded his head in acceptance and followed the *sadhu* back into the cave.

John quickly adapted to his new lifestyle. His day started early with yoga exercises which were taught to him by *Rishi Kripal*. Thereafter, a quick meal of roots, shoots, fruits and exotic herbs collected by the *sadhu,* which were not only extremely nourishing but also invigorating. Most of the day was spent in doing breathing and mind awakening exercises. A quick meal at sunset ended the day. *John*'s body was beginning to get leaner, stronger and flexible. Internally, he was becoming more relaxed, fearless and self-confident. The incessant chatter of his mind was being replaced by calm and stillness bringing with it heightened sense of awareness and incredible abilities of reasoning and intellect. His senses were getting sharper and *John* was transforming both outwardly and internally into a better human being.

When will you teach me the secret skills required to defeat the enemies, *John* asked the *sadhu*. It had been more than three months with hardly any change in the routine. When you are prepared, the *sadhu* replied. But how you will know that I am prepared, *John* asked. I will know, *Rishi Kripal* said and slipped into meditation. *John* grew frustrated and moved out of the cave. The sky was turning dark with black nimbus clouds looming large over the horizon. He started walking aimlessly on the path leading towards the stream, lost in his own thoughts. *John* didn't realize that he had travelled a long distance and the path had bifurcated into a number of smaller paths with each leading in different direction.

John stopped suddenly and looked around. The surroundings looked unfamiliar. He was surrounded by large trees on all sides and the foliage was so thick that he could barely see beyond a few feet. An eerie feeling engulfed him. It was so strong that he felt as if he was about to choke. *John* felt as if a thousand eyes were staring at him. The jungle had suddenly turned into a vast swamp which was swallowing him slowly and the more he struggled, the more was he getting sucked inside the swamp. He could hear strange noises. Noises of wicked laughter, snide remarks and dirty taunts. His entire being felt as if it had been violated and defiled to the core. Fear was coming in waves. *John* wanted to run away from all this, but his legs refused to budge. His breathing was getting constricted and he was gasping for air. Pungent bile rose in his mouth, but he was unable to vomit and was choking. In a flash, *John*'s entire life flashed in front of his eyes. He wanted to shout but no sound came out of his mouth. *John* desperately wanted to die. He wanted the feeling to stop and go away. Darkness swelled in front of his eyes and *John* passed out.

It seemed an eternity when *John* came to his senses. He was in the cave with *Rishi Kripal* by his side. What happened, *John* asked the *sadhu*. How have I reached here? *Rishi Kripal* had a worried look on his face. You ignored my directions and went too far without me. The evil forces followed you and were closing in when I stepped in and intervened. You are safe now. What evil forces, I did not see them, *John* asked. Your eyes are just one of your senses, the *sadhu* replied. Did you feel evil? Definitely yes, replied *John*. It was so terrible that I wished that I die and the torment gets over. It is time that I reveal the message of *Manu* to you and prepare you for the arduous journey ahead, the *sadhu* said.

6

Rishi Kripal was sitting cross legged on the floor. He was in deep thought. *John* waited patiently for him to come out of his trance and tell him the message that *Manu Rishi* had sent for him. What I am about to tell you might surprise you but you need to have faith in me, uttered the *sadhu*. I received a distress call from *Manu* when I was deep in my meditation at *Haridwar*. *Kripal*, he said, "I am sending my friend *John* to you. Train him with all the knowledge that you possess, as he is in grave danger and is being hunted by *Pishach*. I have been able to fight back the initial attack and made *John* escape from here but I fear that I will not be able to hold on any further". Since then, I have tried to establish contact, but have not been successful, *Rishi Kripal* said.

Who is *Pisach*, asked *John*? *Pisach* is the ruler of the underworld, replied the *sadhu*. He is the epitome of evil. Good and evil exist both in this world and the nether world. I do not know what secret you are carrying but one thing is sure that you have made some very deadly enemies. What do you mean by nether world, asked *John*. Son, there are a number of worlds which exist in creation. Earth is just one of them. Like an electron can exist in different states depending on its energy level, similarly a soul can exist in different worlds and in different forms. Science is slowly resolving the dichotomy which exists in the macro and micro model of nature and the Newtonian and Quantum laws of physics. The laws of soul are yet to be explored by modern science. But, the *Hindus* have been working on them since past thousands of years.

Modern science is now stating that at the beginning of the universe, time was just another dimension of space or in other words there was no time as we know of it today. The universe was shrunk to super microscopic levels and only the laws of quantum physics were applicable at that point of time. In a microscopic fraction of time, due to quantum fluctuations, the universe underwent inflation resulting in it being expanded billions of times and giving way to the planets, stars and galaxies as we see today. The *Hindu* scripture *Geeta* says exactly the same. "In the beginning, there was no time. In the blink of an eye, God created the universe". This universe has also a finite life and will also die in the blink of an eye.

The *M Theory* talks of ten dimensions of space with the eleventh dimension of time. Of these, seven dimensions are curled up and make negligible impact on the three major dimensions of length, breadth and height. Quantum theory dictates that at microscopic levels, a particle takes all known paths from a point A to point B in order to undertake a journey from A to B. In fact, the mere act of observing a particle results in it changing its path. All these facts which are recently being discovered were known to ancient *Hindu Rishis*.

What science has not focused on is the spiritual laws of nature which in turn manifest in the present day scientific theories and models.

Gravitation, electromagnetism, strong and weak nuclear forces are the material forces which exist in the universe. Similarly, in the spiritual domain, the forces are love, compassion, faith and intent. The universe is intelligent. Quantum theory has proved time and again that a single particle of energy has intrinsic intelligence in it to decide the path to choose from one point to another and it will change course in case a particular path is closed or open or whether it is being observed or not. Intelligence is intrinsic in the entire fabric of this universe and countless others. The spiritual force which interconnects all animate and inanimate objects is love. Unlike electric charges which repel similar charged particles, strong bonds are formed between objects having mutual love for each other. The more you love, the more will you be loved and more will be the power of love generated within you. Love in spiritual domain can manifest in material domain. If you strongly love a material object, say a car, the stronger will be the possibility of you possessing that car. But here is the caveat; the power of love is directly dependent on the intent of the lover. If the intent is pure and selfless, the power of love increases exponentially. But, if the intent is full of malice and selfish intent, then the power of love diminishes exponentially.

Love manifests into compassion. When you selflessly love a person, you automatically develop a feeling of compassion towards that person. Emotionally you bond with that person and feel her pain, sorrow and joy as your own. You overlook her flaws and do not react even when the other person tries to harm you. The stronger is the power of your love and compassion, the weaker will be the other person's capability to hate you or cause harm to you.

The saying that faith can move mountains is literally true. Faith in the spiritual laws and intrinsic intelligence of nature, own capabilities and in your master and creator must be absolute. There cannot be even an iota of doubt on the intent and capabilities of yourself, your chosen master and the creator. Faith acts as a propelling force which leads to assured fulfillment of desires and goals.

Presently, your mind is in turmoil and untrained. Your powers of love, compassion and faith are low and as a result of which you can be easily harmed and defeated by the evil forces. *Pisach*, the eternal king of all evil will simply devour you. You have a lot to learn and train in very little time. The master then became quiet. Master, *John* asked, you have still not elaborated on who is *Pisach* and what is evil.

The universe is a duality, *Rishi Kripal* said. Here, opposites exist. Like male-female, positive – negative, matter – anti matter. Similarly, in the spiritual plane good exists with evil, love with hatred, fearless with fear, stupidity with intellect, selfless with selfish and so on. *Pisach* is the ruler of evil. It feeds on fear, guilt, greed, malice and vice. All the above mentioned qualities can be present in a being in different measures at different periods of time. When the qualities of fear, greed, vice, guilt and malice are the dominant qualities, then the being possesses evil tendencies and is manipulated by *Pisach*. *Pisach* is on the continuous look out for beings having dominant characteristics of hatred, fear, greed, guilt and vice. It then slowly takes control of them by fuelling their negative traits and coloring their outlook. In the end, the victims become dedicated slaves of *Pisach*; in his complete control, without any realization and lead their entire lives as his followers. If you are once in the grip of *Pisach*, then it is extremely difficult to escape. I don't know who is after you and *Manu Rishi*, but I can definitely tell you that your adversary is filled with hate and revenge and would stop at nothing till either he is no more or you are no more. The option in front of you is clear, kill or get killed. Saying this, *Rishi Kripal* again went into meditation.

John started getting the whole picture. *Kartik*, with his immense hatred and jealousy towards *Chanakya* was an ideal victim for *Pisach*. He would have been made a slave and manipulated to raise an army of *Pisach* followers with a single pointed aim of knowing the secret. By knowing the secret of the nine teams you become stronger and undefeatable. With the knowledge of the secret teams, *Pisach* would then be able to generate intense fear in all beings and manipulate them to join his ranks. Thus, the overall power of *Pisach* would increase and negativity would dominate positivity. People would tend to be fearful, guilty and filled with hatred and vengeance against each other. Good natured persons would be taken advantage off and cheated, the scheming manipulator would rise, and deceit and treachery would be the new traits of mankind. Brother would fight against brother, spouses would be unfaithful, debauchery and gluttony would increase, faith in mankind would be lost and the world would be a truly horrible place to live in. The underworld would rule it.

The grand strategy was now becoming clearer to *John*. Hatred and jealously was fueling intense hatred and jealously. *Pisach* followers after the secret would stop at nothing till they get it. The initial forefathers had literally spawned generations after generations of fanatics who were after the secret and the teams. *John* suddenly realized the enormity of challenges facing him and really missed *Manu Rishi* who was his only partner in this fight against evil.

John decided that he would stop worrying and start acting in this fight against *Pisach*. His first priority was to become strong and have the requisite skill sets required for taking on *Pisach*. He needed to start his training at the earliest. Kindly teach me all that you know and make me capable for my future challenges Master, John addressed *Rishi Kripal* with folded hands and bowed head.

The training was intense and grueling. *John* used to wake up at two in the morning every day after a two hour sleep. Then, for the next four hours he was taught yoga by the master. The ability to make your body strong, flexible and nimble was just one part of the yoga postures and exercises. The real exercises were about control of the body's inner organs. *Rishi Kripal* had told him that there are no involuntary muscles or parts of the human body. A *yogi* is able to regulate each and every part and organ of his body as per his free will. He can increase or decrease his heart rate, body temperature, metabolism and control the functioning of each and every internal organ of his body just like a normal person can control the movement of his arms and legs. That was one of the reasons for *yogis* to survive under extreme and harsh climatic conditions of the Himalayas with no clothes, food, shelter or material comfort for years at an end. There were *yogis* existing who are hundreds of years old and had stopped the process of ageing completely.

Thereafter, *John* was taught about breath and thought control. Like a door gives entry to a house and is selectively opened and shut to regulate the flow of persons entering or exiting the house, similarly our breath and thoughts were the doors to our inner self and needed to be regulated. People who had no control over their breathing and thinking were like palaces with open doors. Anybody could come inside and loot whatever he wanted. Breath and thoughts were the secret entry points of *Pisach*. Once inside, *Pisach* could generate fear, anger, revenge, vice and hatred just by assuming control over the breath and thoughts of a person.

The next part of training involved reading thoughts and emotions of persons. *Rishi Kripal* said that to a trained *yogi* entering a person's inner sanctum through his thoughts and breath was a child's play and once inside, he could easily read what the other person was thinking. It was like gaining an entry into a network once you have got access to administrator privileges and password.

A great deal of training also involved the organization and structures of the multiple worlds that existed. The inhabitants of various worlds, their characteristics and capabilities were taught to *John* in great detail. He was also imparted knowledge on Astral travel and thought communications with beings, animals, trees and plants.

Thereafter, *Rishi Kripal* taught *John* transmutation or transformation of objects from one object to another. He was also taught self-transmutation or changing oneself to any form which one desired at free will.

Towards the end, *John* was taught to meditate and to achieve a deep state of thoughtlessness. The training lasted for almost a year. By the time it was finished *John* was a new being. He became physically very strong and agile and capable of withstanding extreme pain and deprivation. But the real transformation was in his inner self. His mind was calm and still. His thoughts and emotions were measured and under control. There was no fear, anger or jealously against anyone. Instead there was an abundant stream of love and compassion continuously flowing out from his being.

Son, you have been a worthy disciple, *Rishi Kripal* said. I have emptied myself to you and you have absorbed everything like a dry sponge. Now there is nothing left with me to further impart to you. What I have taught you requires a lot of practice before it is perfected. I have shown you the path towards self-actualization and transformation, but you alone have to travel along it. There are no magic chants or quick fix methods of becoming a true *yogi*. It is completely dependent on you and the grace of the almighty creator. My promise to *Manu* has been fulfilled. It is time that we part ways. Remember to always remain guarded. *Pisach* is a master illusionist. His bag of tricks is never empty. One wrong step from your side and he would gain entry into your inner sanctum. I hereby name you *Ajatshatru*, or the one who has conquered his enemies. Roam the world fearlessly and complete your mission in life. Never share your secret with anyone. What I have gifted you are secret knowledge that has been transferred for ages as per ancient *Hindu* traditions of Master – Disciple relations. I forbid you to share this secret with anyone. Always fight evil and protect the innocent.

Ajatshatru realized that the time to bid farewell to his master had come. Your *Dakshina* (Hindu equivalent of fees) Master, he said bowing before *Rishi Kripal* with folded hands. It was customary as part of Master – Disciple tradition, of disciple to give his master a gift of his choosing in return of the education imparted. *Rishi Kripal* became silent. I want you to go to *Dharamsala* where the next part of your journey awaits you. Saying this, he rose from his seat and left the cave never to return. *Ajatshatru* was again left alone.

7

Dharamsala is a quaint old British cantonment situated in *Kangra* district of *Himachal Pradesh*, at an altitude of five thousand feet. The hill station is surrounded by snowcapped peaks on three sides with a deeply wooded valley comprising of oak and conifer forests stretching out in front of the town. Since times immemorial, *Dharamsala* has been ruled by the *Katoach* clan who are said to be the oldest dynasty of the world. The British came in late 1800's with a view of converting *Dharamsala* into their summer capital, but the devastating earthquake of 1905, which almost reduced the town to rubble, made them change their mind and shift the capital to *Simla* instead.

Dharamsala got its brush with destiny when the *Dalai Lama* was invited to settle down in *Mcleodganj* in 1960 after escaping from *Tibet* along with other Tibetan refugees. Today, it's the seat of the Tibetan government in exile and home to a sizeable Tibetan population.

Ajatshatru stood in the middle of the *Kotwali* bazaar slowly taking in his surroundings. In his saffron robe, wooden slippers, unkept hair and beard; he looked like the innumerable *sadhus* and *buddhist* monks who thronged *Dharamsala* enroute to the nearby numerous ancient temples and monasteries. As is customary, food stall owners offer food and shelter to these holy men for free, knowing that they do not have any worldly possession and have faith that the blessings given by the holy men will bring prosperity and well-being to them and their families. In the midst of this sea of humanity, *Ajatshatru* was silently studying his environment. The outwardly charm of the shop keepers, while offering food to the *sadhus* and monks, was in complete contrast with their inner feelings of resentment and sarcasm. He felt suffocated in this continuous whirlpool of incessant thoughts of future, past and present, and emotions of joy, fear, pride, guilt, sorrow, and anger.

Ajatshatru stood transfixed. What a complex net of emotions, beliefs and thoughts we spin for ourselves, he thought. Most of the people were living in their make belief world, attached like leeches to their strong bonds of perceptions, fixed ideas and notions. There was no growth; only death and decay. Life appeared to be a slave of fixed patterns and routine. On the other hand, he marveled at the life being led by the brave *sadhus* and *yogis* who lived like free birds, with a strong belief in their abilities and the will of the creator. No untoward thought, no stress, no worldly possession, yet such a rich and fulfilling life. Living like a lion, roaming the world with no fixed plans and timelines, undertaking adventure and celebrating life with each breath. Deep down, he felt that the creator wanted people to live a joyous and adventurous life and not a life of monotony, fear, anxiety, hatred and routine. Life was a celebration and not a burden.

Ajatshatru wanted to leave the hustle and bustle of the town square and go to some place quieter. He started walking away from the *Kotwali* square towards *Mcleodganj*. The din started receding. As he neared the Buddhist monastery, it became peaceful and quiet. The cosmic sound started reverberating in his ears. *Ajatshatru* felt at peace. *Rishi Kripal* had taught that in the beginning, before the birth of time, there was only sound. The reverberating sound of *Om*. It continues to pervade across all worlds and beings. A *yogi* can continuously hear the cosmic sound and is therefore always connected with the creator and his creation.

The atmosphere in the monastery was quiet and serene. Buddhist monks were sitting in neat rows and reading scriptures. The prayer wheels were in continuous motion and bright colored flags fluttered in the cool breeze. *Ajatshatru* prostrated in front of the golden statue of *Buddha* and after praying for some time moved out to sit in the garden under a tree.

It was almost dark when *Ajatshatru* woke up from his meditation. As he was about to leave, an old monk approached him and said, ‘ It’s getting dark, why don’t you spend the night in the monastery, we would be honored’. *Ajatshatru* bowed to the monk and replied, ‘I have already exceeded my limits as a guest. I am touched by your gesture but I need to go now.’ The old monk remained silent. I will not stop you, he said. May the light of *Buddha* be with you and guide you at every step. *Ajatshatru* again bowed to the monk and left the monastery. He let his heart and feet guide him towards his next destination.

Ajatshatru soon left the lights of *Mcleodganj* behind him and started following a dirt track that was leading towards the mountains. After some time, the track grew narrower and then completely disappeared. He kept on walking in whichever direction his feet took him. *Ajatshatru* was in a trance with no idea of his journey or surroundings. The plains gave way to mountains. It was pitch dark and the mountain side was filled with various noises of nocturnal creatures, but he heard nothing. At daybreak, *Ajatshatru* suddenly stopped. He was standing in the middle of a clearing deep inside a jungle which was surrounded by mountains from all sides. Standing next to him was a small boy of around six years in a monk's robes with a small G*addi* pup, which was the local breed of mountain dog and was widely domesticated by the nomadic community of *Dharamsala*.

Ajatshatru was taken aback. Who are you and what are you doing here, he asked the boy. Sir, I am *Satvik*, an orphan adopted by the monastery and this is my pet dog *Moti*. Yesterday, as you left the monastery, I was playing outside with *Moti*. Suddenly, I had this strange urge to follow you. So, we both started following you and here we are. But where are we, *Ajatshatru* asked. I don't know, the boy replied. It was pitch dark and you were walking cross country the whole night. We kept on following you as we did not want to get lost.

Ajatshatru looked around his surroundings. The clearing was roughly rectangular with deep and thick jungle on all sides. Snowcapped Himalayan peaks encircled the complete landscape. Where have I landed myself and these two strangers now, he thought. After some time, *Ajatshatru* addressed *Satvik*. It seems that we need to temporarily construct a shelter in this clearing till such time I figure out a way of getting us out. I want you and *Moti* to help me. Both of you will not leave this clearing without me and would obey whatever I tell you. Hooray, *Satvik* shouted with joy with *Moti* strongly wagging his tail in agreement.

The three of them started their task in real earnest. They had soon collected a lot of dry and solid logs and branches. With creepers and vines, *Ajatshatru* was able to tie up logs together to construct a makeshift shelter to protect them from the elements. A nearby mountain stream provided them with fresh and clean water and with the knowledge gained from his stay with *Rishi Kripal*, *Ajatshatru* was able to light a fire as well as gather jungle fruits, roots, herbs and leaves which constituted the basic diet for them. Both *Satvik* and *Moti* turned out to be real assets. Not only was *Satvik* used to a rugged and hard life but also possessed a natural instinct of living in jungles and was a great help to *Ajatshatru* in establishing the camp, collecting water, gathering food, lighting fire and creating basic tools and implements. *Moti* was an effective guide cum guard who ensured that the nocturnal creatures were kept at bay when *Ajatshatru* and *Satvik* slept at night.

As time passed, *Ajatshatru*, *Satvik* and *Moti* settled down to their new life. *Ajatshatru* had reasoned that till now, he was always being guided along his journey. It would be futile to go searching for the nine teams, *Rishi Kripal* or *Manu Rishi*. There was always a hidden meaning in his master's words and he was sure that the three of them were not in this situation by chance. There had to be a higher purpose which he did not know now, but was sure that it would be revealed to him when the time was right.

The day started early, before sun rise. While *Ajatshatru* did strenuous yoga exercises, *Moti* and *Satvik* would go to the stream to get water and also pick up dry branches on the way back. Then, *Ajatshatru* would go and collect fruits, herbs, roots and other edible stuff from the forest. After an early breakfast, *Satvik* would clean the camp while *Moti* stood guard. *Ajatshatru* had created a small raised platform at the base of a nearby banyan tree and would spend hours meditating and practicing the techniques taught by *Rishi Kripal*. Though in theory, he knew everything, but realizing it in reality was a different story which could only be possible with hard work, practice and grace. The later part of the afternoon was spent in having an early dinner and preparing for the night.

At night, everything changed. The forest came alive from a large variety of noises. The trees took eerie shapes and it seemed as if the branches were closing up on them. The rustling of leaves could imply anything from wind, insect, snake or other forms of slithering creatures which only came out during the night. *Satvik* had fabricated a makeshift drum out of the hollow trunk of a tree and used it effectively to create a deep sound that had managed to keep predators at bay, till now. Both, *Ajatshatru* and *Satvik* slept in shifts, with one keeping watch while the other slept.

Initially, *Ajatshatru* was very sincere and dedicated towards yoga and meditation. But, with each passing day he started getting frustrated and complacent. In theory, the concept of keeping your mind still appeared to be simple, but in practice, the harder he tried, the more thoughts emerged. Sometimes, doubts rose on his own decisions regarding the path that he had chosen and promised to follow. Were the nine teams actually present? Where was *Muni Rishi* and what happened to him? Why did *Rishi Kripal* leave him? What was he doing in this isolated place? The stream of thoughts was endless. Each time these thoughts surfaced, *Ajatshatru* would contemplate on them with the purpose of voluntarily preventing them from entering his subconscious mind. Through yoga, he would first regulate his breathing and calm down. Thereafter, sitting in the lotus position, he would contemplate on the thought and become the silent witness to it. He started treating the thought as a guest. Like a guest, it was given due importance and freedom to do whatever it wanted to do or go wherever it wanted to go. *Ajatshatru,* as a perfect host, did not interrupt or ignore it, but just dispassionately observed it. Slowly but surely the stream of thoughts entering his mind subsided.

And then the rains came and changed everything. It rained continuously for three days. Everything got drenched. The make shift shelter got washed away and *Ajatshatru*, *Satvik* and *Moti* huddled close to each other and took shelter underneath the banyan tree. They had not eaten, drank or slept for two days and were completely exhausted. There was no question of yoga and meditation. It appeared as if Mother Nature was mocking *Ajatshatru* and taunting him. It was a battle between the mind and the body and it was quite evident that the body had an upper hand. *Ajatshatru* was becoming more and more irritable and angry and was picking faults in *Satvik* and *Moti*. *Satvik*, in his eagerness to please *Ajatshatru* went out with *Moti* to the jungle to get some food and fresh water.

In the evening, *Ajatshatru* became worried when *Satvik* did not return back to the clearing. He cursed himself for giving vent to his frustration and irritation on the little boy who was not responsible for their present predicament. I just hope that *Satvik* is not lost or in grave trouble; such and numerous other thoughts were crossing *Ajatshatru*'s mind with each passing moment. It was getting dark and in a few moments, the entire place would be filled with darkness. Then it would be almost impossible to even go out and look for *Satvik* and *Moti*. '*Satvik, Moti*', *Ajatshatru* screamed. He was shouting at the top of his voice and getting hysterical. He feared that incase he left the clearing to go and look out for *Satvik* and *Moti* and they returned back then finding him missing maybe they would again leave the clearing.

Evening turned into night but *Satvik* and *Moti* did not return. The usually calm and composed *Ajatshatru* was a picture of fear and despair. Over the days, since he had met *Satvik* and *Moti*, *Ajatshatru* had started to like them and a deep bond of friendship and companionship had developed amongst them. Now, his only two friends in the entire world were missing and he was sitting all alone in the clearing with rain beating down mercilessly on him and night engulfing him in its fold. Oh my God, what have I done! *Ajatshatru* cried in deep remorse. He had forgotten that it was raining and that he had not slept or eaten for days. All that *Ajatshatru* remembered was that his only two friends and companions were lost and he was to be blamed for it. Grief overtook *Ajatshatru* and he collapsed unconscious to the ground, a tired and broken man.

When *Ajatshatru* woke up, it was daybreak. It was still raining and there was no sign of *Satvik* and *Moti*. He decided to leave the clearing in search of his friends. '*Satvik Moti*', he shouted and started walking into the jungle. He initially went to the nearby stream from where they used to collect water and thereafter to the nearby places from where the three of them used to collect fruits and herbs for their daily needs. On not finding *Satvik* and *Moti* at the above places, *Ajatshatru* entered the thick jungle. He was determined and filled with a purpose to locate and bring back *Satvik* and *Moti* at any cost.

In his zeal to locate *Satvik* and *Moti*, *Ajatshatru* strayed deep inside the jungle. After a long and hectic search, he sat down on a rock tired and dejected. His whole body had become weak from not eating for a long time and the lack of success in finding *Satvik* and *Moti* had de motivated him. He started to doubt his plan. What if *Satvik* had made up his mind to ditch me in the rain and strike out on his own along with *Moti*; What if both of them were presently in the clearing looking for me while I am here all alone and lost in this jungle; How will I be able to get out alive from here; such and numerous other questions were constantly tormenting him. Deep down a voice was saying; why you don't rest for some time, look out for a clearing, built another shelter and get on with life. Your main purpose was to locate and protect the nine teams and not *Satvik* and *Moti*. They both were mere distractions. Contradictory thoughts were crowding *Ajatshatru*'s mind making him confused and indecisive.

Ajatshatru decided to continue his search for *Satvik* and *Moti*. He realized that he needed to get out of the valley and climb the mountains in order to get a better view. Since, he was surrounded by mountains on all sides; he decided to climb the nearest one as it also looked to be the smallest one with gentle slope leading towards the summit. The climb was tiring and arduous, but by night fall, *Ajatshatru* was able to reach the summit. Once on the top, he had a bird's eye view of his surroundings. As far as his gaze would go, there were ranges after ranges of mountains behind him with a large glacier flowing in between the ranges. Ahead of him, the jungle spread out with mountains on all sides. There was no smoke and no sign of civilization. '*Satvik, Moti*', *Ajatshatru* shouted himself hoarse but there was no response. He decided to spend the night at the summit and renew his search the next day in the morning. Thankfully, the rains had stopped and a clear moon lit night afforded him a great deal of visibility. It was getting chilly. Nights on mountains were very unpredictable and could change from good to worse in a matter of minutes.

Ajatshatru started searching for a shelter to protect him from the elements during the night. After descending a few steps, he discovered a small fold in the ground. He huddled inside and decided to regulate his body temperature by yoga. *Rishi Kripal* had taught him that it was possible to increase or lower the body temperature by yoga. Though, *Ajatshatru* knew the technique but was unable to regulate his body temperature during his previous attempts while learning with the master. Once again, he deliberately focused on all the nuances of the posture and with controlled breath and single pointed concentration went over the entire process of temperature regulation. Suddenly, lo and behold, a wave of intense warmth spread through his entire being, as if somebody had thrown a thick blanket over him. Thereafter, *Ajatshatru* was easily able to spend the night. For the first time he realized that what he was taught by his master was possible, but could only be achieved by single pointed concentration and practice.

At daybreak, *Ajatshatru* started exploring his surroundings. He saw a mound of earth which almost resembled that of a person sitting in lotus position. On closer inspection, *Ajatshatru* was shocked to discover that the mound of earth was in fact a naked *sadhu* sitting cross legged in deep meditation. The *sadhu* must have been sitting in this posture for a very long time because grass and shrub had grown all around him. An ant hill had grown over the *sadhu*'s body and the army of ants was busy scurrying up and down his body. In spite of being still like a statue, the *sadhu* was not dead. The body had not decayed; in fact it appeared to be taut and fresh. The *yogi*'s face was expressionless and eyes semi closed. He was definitely in a different world and was a living proof that whatever *Rishi Kripal* had taught was achievable by anyone and everyone. *Ajatshatru* bowed his head in reverence to the noble soul and continued his journey in search of *Satvik* and *Moti*.

Ajatshatru surveyed the underlying valley and decided to retrace his steps towards the clearing. This time, he chose a different route. After descending the mountain, he started moving towards the mountain stream. At a distance, he found a pack of wild dogs fighting with each other over a piece of meat. *Ajatshatru* rushed towards them with arms outstretched and shouting at the top of his voice. Seeing him charging towards them, the pack disappeared into the jungle leaving behind the piece of meat over which they were fighting. As *Ajatshatru* moved closer he was horrified and filled with shock on seeing that the piece of meat over which the wild dogs were fighting was the hind leg of *Moti*. Realizing that *Satvik* and *Moti* were in mortal danger, *Ajatshatru* started moving in circles around the place where he had discovered Moti's leg, shouting at the top of his voice. At a distance, he stumbled upon the mangled remains of *Moti*. It was quite evident that he had a terrible death. Someone had systematically severed each portion of his limbs one after the other and left him to die a slow and painful death with wild animals chewing at his remains. A chill ran down *Ajatshatru*'s spine. *Satvik*, he shouted at the top of his voice and suddenly stumbled onto the ground after hitting a protruding object covered with grime and mud. Vomit rose through *Ajatshatru*'s stomach. The protruding object was the head of *Satvik*. Someone had buried him neck down in the ground and had then suffocated him by piling mud and dirt over his head after torturing him. His whole face was cut, burnt and totally disfigured. It would have been a suffocating and painful death. *Ajatshatru* was filled with fear and rage and he knelt down and frantically started removing the dirt and mud from *Satvik*'s mortal remains. As he cleared the mud from *Satvik*'s head, he was aghast to find that his tormentors had tonsured his head and had branded it with the symbol. 🜏 ; the alchemist symbol of decay. *Ajatshatru* suddenly felt a suffocating feeling of panic overcoming him. His enemies had discovered him and were lying in wait for him.

8

The pineal gland, also known as the pineal body, *Conarium* or *Epiphysis Cerebri*, is a small endocrine gland in the vertebrate brain. Its shape resembles a tiny pine cone (hence its name), and it is located in the *Epithalamus*, near the centre of the brain, between the two hemispheres, tucked in a groove where the two halves of the thalamus join. Dr. Rick Strassman, who conducted research on the psychedelic Dimethyltryptamine (DMT) in the 1990s at the University of New Mexico, has speculated that the pineal gland plays a role in the production of DMT in the human brain. Strassman also states that the human pineal gland is not actually part of the brain. He explains that the gland develops from specialized tissues in the roof of the fetal mouth, where it then migrates to the center of the brain as the brain develops further. The pineal gland is the only un-paired organ deep in the brain. It becomes visible in the developing fetus at forty-nine days after conception. This is also the time in which one can clearly see an indication of either a female or male gender. Coincidentally, *Buddhists* believe that the soul is reincarnated within forty-nine days as well.

The *Hindus* and *Buddhists* have long believed that the physical route to the spiritual world goes through the pineal gland. It is also referred to as the third eye. While the external pair of eyes is meant to see outwards, the third eye is meant to see inwards. By yoga and meditation, the third eye can be awakened and once awakened, the person has unlimited access to the physical as well as spiritual world. The third eye is depicted in the statues of *Hindu* God *Shiva* and the tip of *Buddha*'s head has a cone exactly similar in shape to the pineal gland and symbolizes the entry point of the spiritual world with the physical world.

Ajatshatru realized that he was dealing with a highly dangerous and accomplished enemy who was deliberately not killing him. In the present state and circumstances, he was unable to even detect him, leave alone destroy him. He needed to get help from his masters, either *Muni Rishi* or *Rishi Kripal* and there was no other option left but to contact them on the spiritual plane through astral travel. The only hitch was that though in theory he knew everything about the various spiritual levels and worlds and the technique of astral travel, but he had no practical experience. Time had come to do or die. He had to master the technique of astral travel. His life depended on it.

Ajatshatru found a big pine tree and after clearing its surroundings, he sat down underneath it to meditate. Initially, he did the *yoga* exercises taught to him to regulate his breathing and calm his mind. Thereafter, by chanting secret hymns, *Ajatshatru* was able to create a protective astral sphere around his physical body which would guard it during the deep state of meditation when the soul would leave the body for astral travel and would be connected to it by only a single spiritual astral thread. As taught by *Rishi Kripal*, *Ajatshatru* started the process of meditation by visualizing the end state of him having a meeting with *Rishi Muni* and *Rishi Kripal* on a spiritual plane through astral travel. *Rishi Kripal* had taught him that in order to have a successful astral travel, the visualization needs to be in great detail. A detailed image of the meeting along with its surroundings would make astral travel easier and faster. After visualizing his meeting with the masters, *Ajatshatru* sat down in the lotus position with his spine erect to ensure a smooth passage of cosmic energy from the base of his spine to the universal source. Then, concentrating on the tip of his nose, he started chanting the secret hymn and concentrating on the sound produced by the syllables. It is said that when you are able to resonate in synch with the frequency of the cosmic sound, then you enter the spiritual plane. In the spiritual plane, your abilities become boundless. You can create whatever you want, travel back and forth in time, experience different worlds, meet whoever you wish to meet...The list is endless. The *Hindus* believe in the law of conservation of spiritual energy which means that the sum total of souls in the universe remains constant. Souls are continuously dying and then being reborn. They are on a never ending journey of birth and death with only a few, who have managed to reach the zenith of spirituality, achieving the state of *Nirvana* (Salvation) and merging with the cosmic sound.

Ajatshatru had soon reached a state of thoughtlessness and had no outward feeling of his body. He then suddenly experienced being lifted up from his body and like a low cloud passing over the mountains, floating over it, which was still sitting erect in the lotus position under the pine tree. The feeling was ecstatic and exciting and *Ajatshatru* could not control it. He felt a sudden thud and was transported back inside his body. Oh! He exclaimed. I have actually been outside my body and the whole experience is so liberating. I now need to learn to keep my emotions in check and not get too much excited. He again sat down in meditation.

After a number of hits and misses, *Ajatshatru* was able to float over his body in the astral plane. He could observe that he was attached to his body by the astral thread and till such time the thread remained connected with the body, he would be able to come back to it. *Ajatshatru* was now among the very few people who had a first-hand experience of witnessing the soul separate from the body during their lifetime.

Ajatshatru thought of his meeting with *Rishi Kripal* and was immediately transported to the depth of a cave where the *sadhu* was sitting in lotus position and waiting for him. So I see that my disciple has mastered the art of astral travel, he said. It has been made possible only due to your blessings, *Ajatshatru* replied. Tell me what brings you here, the master asked. *Ajatshatru* narrated the entire chain of events right from his landing up at *Dharamsala* to the horrible discovery of the mortal remains of *Satvik* and *Moti* with the branding on *Satvik*'s head.

The moment has come much before than I visualized, *Rishi Kripal* said. Which moment master, *Ajatshatru* asked. Your coming face to face with *Pisach* is inevitable. The curse of the secrets was transferred to you by *Muni Rishi* and therefore *Pisach* is coming after you. *Ajatshatru* grew silent. What curse master, he finally asked. You see, in *Hindus* the lineage flows from father to son and from master to disciple. By accepting me as your master, you and I have chosen by our free will to interlink our destinies. Similarly, by telling you the secret and your acceptance to be a part of the arrangement, have also by free will, interlinked yours and *Manu Rishi*'s destinies. The linkages formed by free will are much more strong and powerful as compared to the linkages formed by nature. By exercising their free will, the persons have over ruled the destiny decided by nature. Ancient scriptures regularly quote that the entire creation is a massive illusion and we are just playing our role in this epic theatre. However, the only difference is that each soul has the power to change his role and alter the play in real time by exercising his free will. When you exercise your free will, then the play starts unfolding based on your choices and paths, which in turn make you the direct beneficiary of your gains and losses and the cycle of *karma* starts afresh.

The master paused for some time and then continued. The secret that *Manu Rishi* has shared with you is so powerful that it has the potential to change the world. That is the reason why *Pisach* is after you and will stop at nothing till he finishes you. The curse of the secret is that whoever knows the secret has to live a life of struggle till the very end and will not die a natural death. *Manu Rishi* had warned me when he was about to reveal the secret about the consequences and I accepted it, *Ajatshatru* said. Also, you have cleared my doubts concerning death hence I am not bothered whether I die a natural or a horrible death. *Pisach* cannot touch my true essence, my soul, till such time I do not surrender to him and that I am never going to do, *Ajatshatru* added. *Rishi Kripal* smiled. I expected this answer from you, my son, he said. *Ajatshatru* touched his feet and said, guide me my master, what should I do now. Time is less and I have not mastered most of the things that you have taught me. There are no fixed recipes for this challenge, *Rishi Kripal* replied. You have to find your own way. But I can surely advise you to use this medium of astral travel, which you have mastered, to contact any of the teams for assistance.

Ajatshatru woke up with a start. Was I actually having a conversation with *Rishi Kripal* or was I just dreaming, he said to himself. Knowing that *Pisach* was on his heels, *Ajatshatru* decided to move away from his location to somewhere safe. He needed time to chalk out a plan to defeat *Pisach*. The mountain top would give him a clearer view of the surrounding areas so he decided to first move there. From the top, *Ajatshatru* could make out the faint outline of a mountain stream in the far distance. He decided to go to a place near the river and search for a suitable shelter. On reaching the stream, *Ajatshatru* decided to create a small shelter on a tree, a kind of tree house. This would keep him safe from the nocturnal predators and would also afford him an opportunity to practice meditation unhindered. He found an old tree near the bank of the stream and made a makeshift shelter between its branches at a height of ten feet.

Honing his skills at meditation and astral travel became the foremost priority for *Ajatshatru*. It was relatively simpler to meditate during periods of quiet and peace but the real challenge lay in going into the deep state of thoughtlessness when there was noise or he was thirsty, hungry or in pain. Fear too was a major impediment to successful meditation as it generated a series of thoughts which became very difficult to control. Slowly, *Ajatshatru* was able to train his mind to control and regulate the thoughts emanating from it.

Ajatshatru decided to meditate on the symbol 🜏 which was engraved on *Satvik*'s skull. He wanted to explore the region of *Pisach* and gauge his opponent's strength. The moment he reached a state of thoughtlessness, *Ajatshatru* was pulled inside a dark region almost against his wishes. There was darkness all around and the stench was unbearable. An overpowering smell of decay, rotting flesh and human excreta was all around him. Slowly, he started hearing the deep throated voices of people in fear, panic and pain. It seemed as if a large number of persons had been subjected to some grave torture and they were continuously begging and crying for mercy. As his vision adjusted to the dark world, *Ajatshatru* witnessed a horrible sight which ran a deep chill down his spine. Below him was a sea of human flesh and excreta; of pile upon pile of dead people, and inside this sea were thousands and thousands of people crying, wailing and begging for mercy. Suddenly, *Ajatshatru* experienced a strong pull pulling him inside this vortex of human death and decay. The smell, vision and voices had already drowned his senses and in spite of his best efforts, he started experiencing panic and fear building up inside. As the intensity of panic increased, *Ajatshatru* started losing control over his emotions and thoughts and started falling faster into the centre of the vortex. As a last ditch effort, *Ajatshatru* remembered his master's teaching that you and you alone are the master of your mind. It cannot be surrendered to be controlled by anyone else. He resolved his will power and asserted his control over his mind. After some time, he experienced the pull receding and the horrible emotions leaving him. *Ajatshatru*, thereafter was able to witness the scene as an observer and not as a participant. After some time, *Ajatshatru* returned back from his astral journey into his physical body. He was weak and sweating from this difficult ordeal. It took a while for the shivering to go away. The experience had given him an insight into his enemy's world and powers and he was not yet ready to take him on.

Ajatshatru grew more determined after witnessing a portion of his opponent's world. He realized that he was ill prepared to take on *Pisach* and his army of followers at the present moment. *Ajatshatru* decided to analyze *Pisach*'s strengths and weaknesses and evolve a strategy to defeat him. He realized that *Pisach* had some great strength. First, it was able to locate him in all corners of the world. Escaping from his surveillance was very difficult. Secondly, *Pisach* could easily travel through different worlds as his real kingdom lay in the nether world, a world that was dark and terrible and he had witnessed a small portion of it, just now. Thirdly, *Pisach* could easily enter a person's mind and generate fear, panic, anger and revenge. This ultimately resulted in the person becoming a prey of *Pisach*. Lastly, *Pisach* had the strength and capability to harm you in different worlds and in different states; physical, astral and emotional.

Ajatshatru also realized, that in all cases, *Pisach* wanted to gain control by first targeting the mind and the thoughts being generated. If he could gain total control over his thoughts and feelings, it would be very difficult for *Pisach* to harm him or take control over him. He also realized that *Pisach* had always found him out when he was not in control of his thoughts. It appeared as if *Pisach* was tuning in to the millions of thoughts being generated across different worlds and using them to identify his victim and home on to them. Maybe, it was he who had led *Pisach* into *Manu Rishi*'s cave. He also realized that a strong belief in yourself and in your spiritual master was able to wean off Pisach's influence.

Ajatshatru decided that he needed to be physically, mentally, emotionally, spiritually and intellectually very strong before even thinking of taking on *Pisach*. He needed to guard his thoughts very carefully or else he would give out his location. There was no time to be lost. *Ajatshatru* had to find a secluded place where he could train and hone his skills. Wasting no more time, he started walking towards the peaks. The mountains will provide me with a safe place away from the preying eyes of *Pisach*, *Ajatshatru* realized.

Soon *Ajatshatru* reached a safe place in the mountains where he could practice and hone his skills. To increase his physical strength and stamina, he started practicing various yoga postures and exercises that were taught by *Rishi Kripal* to increase his strength, flexibility and agility. Soon, he was able to lift heavy loads and march continuously for days at a stretch. His body became extremely flexible and he was able to easily climb trees and jump across branches and obstacles like a monkey. He was able to control his breathing and body temperature to such an extent that he could survive extreme heat and biting cold without wearing any clothes and stay underwater for minutes without breathing. By having an effective control over his metabolism, *Ajatshatru* could control hunger and thirst and stay without food and water for days at a stretch. But the biggest achievement was in his mental, spiritual and emotional state. There were no second thoughts about his abilities. *Ajatshatru* now possessed strong will power and self-belief. His faith in his master was absolute. No longer were his emotions slave to situations and circumstances but were loyal servants to his mind. He was now able to quickly reach a state of deep meditation and stay thoughtless for days at a stretch. He was able to astral travel between different worlds at will. There was no fear, anger, jealousy or want, but a deep feeling of love and compassion. He was no longer afraid of or revengeful towards *Pisach*.

He understood the co-existence of good and evil, black and white... his fight was against evil with no malice towards the perpetrator.

Outwardly, *Ajatshatru* was not growing old. Though his surroundings were constantly changing and going through the various cycles of birth and death, *Ajatshatru* remained unchanged. By meditating for long stretches in a state of total thoughtlessness he was becoming impervious to entropy; there was no decay. Time now was just another dimension in a particular world. Death, the way we understand it, could not touch him. He had moved beyond the human state of birth and death...

Once, when *Ajatshatru* was in a deep state of meditation, he became aware of continuous cries of help coming from an unknown source. He could sense a beautiful place surrounded by lofty mountains and nestled along the banks of a lake having crystal clear blue water. The voices were coming from a small settlement of thatched huts just adjacent to the lake. Initially, the settlement appeared to be deserted but the voices seemed to come from inside one of the thatched huts. Inside the hut, around ten men, women and children were huddled around a round table and looking intently at a pitcher of water. The color of water was slowly turning blood red from crystal clear blue. Help! *Ajatshatru*, come fast... they all were shouting.

9

Ajatshatru came out of his trance. He instinctively knew that one of the secret teams was in trouble and he needed to get to them fast. He would reach till them by following his instincts. The long hours of meditation and absolute thought control had made him acutely aware of his surroundings. Like a flock of Siberian cranes that migrate over thousands of kilometers every year to the same place in India, *Ajatshatru* was now capable of navigating by instinct to any corner of the world. He no longer needed directions.

After a strenuous journey of four days through deep forests, treacherous rivers and steep mountains, *Ajatshatru* was standing at the base of a huge waterfall. The water from the river was falling from a height of two hundred feet, getting collected in a natural bowl and thereafter falling down into the deep valley below. The scene was so terrifying that no person in his sane mind would ever attempt to cross the waterfall from the small ledge where he was standing; midway between the mountain top and the valley floor. The water was flowing swiftly and making eddies as it circled and swept down into the valley. *Ajatshatru* took one step forward and entered the deep swirling water. Surprisingly, at the exact spot where he was standing, water was absolutely calm and knee deep. *Ajatshatru* started walking slowly forward and entered the waterfall. Behind the enormous wall of fast flowing water was a small tunnel, totally hidden from view from outside. He entered the tunnel and after a while came out through the other side.

Ajatshatru was standing on a ledge overlooking a beautiful valley surrounded by mountains from all sides. Below him, on the valley floor was a beautiful lake having crystal blue water and nestled around one corner of the lake were a few thatched huts. *Ajatshatru* had reached the location of the first secret team. He quickly moved down the ledge into the valley and after walking along the lake reached the village. A strange sight greeted him.

The village was entirely uninhabited. There was not a soul in sight. *Ajatshatru* slowly entered the village and after encircling the houses entered the first hut. Though outwardly the huts looked fragile, but once inside, he realized that the outward appearance was a deception. The huts were made of an unknown material which was light as well as strong. The hut had two small rooms. After searching the hut and finding no one inside, *Ajatshatru* entered the second hut and then the third and so on. After searching the whole village, *Ajatshatru* stood at the bank of the lake wondering where the inhabitants of the village were. Suddenly, a huge underwater vessel emerged from the depth of the lake and stood opposite him. The vessel was shaped like a sphere having partial glass windows. He could make out people dressed in white robes standing inside the vessel and looking at him. After a while, the hatch at the top of the vessel opened and an old man in white robes stepped outside and stood next to him.

Greetings my friend, the old man said. You must be the savior chosen by *Manu Rishi*. *Ajatshatru* introduced himself and gave out the circumstances which had led him to this exotic place. By this time, the other persons had alighted from the vessel and were standing excitedly around him. The mysterious vessel again vanished inside the lake without making a splash. In all, the mysterious place had six men, four women and three children. The old man who spoke to *Ajatshatru* appeared to be the leader of the group. Why have I been summoned, *Ajatshatru* asked. It's a long story, the old man replied. Let us go inside and I will tell you everything in detail. Saying this, the old man led *Ajatshatru* by hand into the nearest hut.

Once inside, everybody got seated around a big circular table and the women folk first offered *Ajatshatru* a refreshing drink which appeared to be made of some exotic herbs along with fresh fruit. Kindly eat, the old man said. You must be tired after undertaking such a long journey. Once everybody had settled down and had something to eat and drink, the old man started speaking in a low and gentle voice.

We are the alchemy team, he said. Many years ago, we were sent by *Chanakya* to this place as it was feared that our knowledge could fall on wrong hands and be misused against the overall good of mankind. Since then, we have never ventured outside this self-sustaining eco system nor has anyone from the outside world visited us… till now. But I have come on your request, *Ajatshatru* said. I was not referring to you when I made the last statement, the old man said in a grave voice. *Ajatshatru* became silent.

This valley is perpetually covered by a thick layer of clouds round the year making it impossible to be identified from air. The mountains all around have extremely steep slopes and have multiple ranges with deep ravines and thick valleys making it impossible for even the animals to cross over to this side. The only feasible route of entry is through which you have come and that too can only be accessed in case you are exactly aware of where to stand on the ledge beneath the waterfall. One wrong step would take you to your death hundreds of meters down in the valley. To be sure that no one comes inside; we have set up a series of traps and sensors to immediately inform us in case there is an intrusion. One of the ways is that we test the water of the lake with a special chemical which changes its color to scarlet red as soon as any stranger enters the lake. For the first time since we have migrated to this place, the color of chemical has turned red after reacting with the lake's water, thereby indicating that a stranger has entered our secret haven and is presently on the lookout for the secret that can change the entire fabric of human civilization.

What secret, *Ajatshatru* enquired from the old man. The secret of alchemy or the transmutation of elements, the old man replied. He paused for a while and then continued. As you are aware, the metals which exhibit high anti rust and anti-corrosion properties like gold and silver are known as noble metals. History is replete with instances wherein people have attempted to convert base metals like lead into noble metals like gold. Our team is not only capable of converting base metal into noble metals but also of giving any metal any chosen property. We can make iron, corrosion and rust free and as malleable as gold. Or we can give gold the strength of graphene and the property of rust and corrosion. Thus, there is no requirement of using a particular metal for a particular task; like making sophisticated machinery out of titanium or platinum. The properties of iron can be suitably modified to fit into the requirements of any task. This ensures a limitless availability of natural resource which can be suitably modified to be capable of performing any specified task.

Ajatshatru was stunned. In all probability, the iron pillar of *Qutab* must have been made by the alchemy team; a secret reminder to the world of the enormous power it possessed. He now understood that the material which was used to construct the houses and the underwater vessel was unique and possessed strange properties. The knowledge of the alchemy team could transform the world in unimaginable ways. This is phenomenal, he said. Why don't you share your discovery with the rest of the world? We will, when the time is right, the old man replied. What you mean by this, Ajatshatru asked.

The world is undergoing great upheaval as we speak. The powers of *Pisach* and his followers have increased exponentially. The struggle between good and evil has reached epic proportions and sadly, evil appears to have the edge over good. We can only share our knowledge on the directions of the wise men and they have forbidden us to share the secret at the present moment. Who are the wise men, *Ajatshatru* asked? The wise men are a group of seven *Rishis* living in different worlds. They have supernatural powers and have defeated death. They can assume any form and are part of the creation's intrinsic intelligence. Nothing is hidden from them. The wise men are fully aware of the powers of *Pisach* and the ongoing battle between good and evil but they do not intervene till such time the entire creation is threatened and is about to be disintegrated into utter chaos and disharmony. They intervened during the epic churning of the seas to extract the secret nectar of life, millions of years ago and may intervene now. Is *Manu Rishi* also part of the wise men, *Ajatshatru* asked? The old man nodded in affirmative. *Manu Rishi* has identified you amongst millions to fight against *Pisach* and his army. There must be some exceptional qualities in you that you have been chosen as the savior of the secret society, the old man said. There is no time to be wasted, he added and glanced towards the pitcher. The water of the pitcher was fast turning into red.

Ajatshatru realized that he had very less time to find out the intruder and deal with him. It was also important that the secret of material transformation and the members of the secret society were protected and made safe, so that he could pursue the intruder unhindered. Where are your laboratories and the secret formula for material transformation, *Ajatshatru* asked the old man.

The process of material transformation is carried out over nine different steps. One of the essential elements in the transformation is the celestial dust of a meteorite which had fallen here millions of years ago. The laboratories and the meteorite are located under water and can only be accessed by the special craft which has been specially developed for this purpose, the team leader said. I need to first ensure the safety of the team and laboratory before I take on the intruder, *Ajatshatru* replied. The meteorite is safely kept in a hidden storage vault inside the laboratory complex, the old man said. The laboratory also is secured via multiple layers of security and difficult to access. *Ajatshatru* decided to let the team move to the underwater laboratory and stay there while he tracked down the intruder on land. Once the threat has been eliminated, the team could surface safely.

I would like to escort the team to the laboratory and after being satisfied with the security set up would then surface to deal with the intruder, *Ajatshatru* said to the old man. Very well, the old man said. Call the craft; we have no time to waste. Immediately the entire team along with *Ajatshatru* moved out of the hut and started walking towards the lake where the underwater craft was standing ready to take them to their destination.

The underwater craft was a marvel of engineering. Never before in his life had *Ajatshatru* seen such a beautiful and extremely hi tech machine. Unlike a submarine, which is cigar shaped; the vessel was spherical and almost floating on the lake's surface. Inside, the entire surface was made of a transparent material affording 360 degree view all around. The team was seated around the walls of the vessel at the top level while the navigation and propulsion systems were beneath. Within no time, the craft was drawing in water into its lower chambers and submerging fast. Once fully submerged, the vessel started moving towards the bottom of the lake at a fast speed. There was no noise and *Ajatshatru* wondered how such a massive craft was being driven at such a speed. The vessel is being driven by atomic power, the old man said seeing the look of astonishment on *Ajatshatru*'s face. We are taking in water and breaking it into hydrogen and oxygen. The energy released in this reaction is being used to propel the craft while the oxygen is used for circulation inside the vessel.

The lake was very deep. After a while, the craft entered a narrow trench. The trench initially went straight down and thereafter veered towards the top until it was almost running parallel to the lake bed. Suddenly, the craft started releasing water from its chambers and began surfacing. A strange sight greeted *Ajatshatru*. The craft was floating inside a huge cavern at the floor of the lake. The cavern stretched as far as the eyes could see. The hatch of the vessel opened and the members alighted from it and moved towards the cavern. The area was well lit by mysterious lights running all along the roof of the cavern. Let's move, the old man said, once *Ajatshatru* and all the team members had alighted from the vessel.

The party reached the laboratory complex after walking through a narrow tunnel. Like any modern lab, it housed a number of rooms with sophisticated machinery. Towards the end was a double locked door, probably the place where the meteoroid dust was kept. We are safe here, the team leader said. This place has been specifically built with the purpose of secrecy and safety. Well then I shall leave, *Ajatshatru* said. The vessel has been programmed to take you ashore. We will be monitoring our sensors and would immediately come to know when the intruder has been eliminated, the team leader said. The task ahead is full of peril and challenges. As a team we are grateful to you for coming to our rescue. This is our last meeting. It was a pleasure knowing you, the leader added. *Ajatshatru* gave one long look at the complex and personally went and said goodbye to each member of the team. He was indeed fortunate to have been chosen by *Manu Rishi* for such an important task. His journey till now had been really fascinating and full of mystery and adventure. After a while, *Ajatshatru* boarded the vessel and started his return journey to the shore.

Ajatshatru was shocked as soon as he reached the shore. The whole forest was ablaze with flames touching the sky. The air was thick with smoke and the shrieks of monkeys and frightened chatter of birds rendered the atmosphere. The huts were fire resistant and stood unaffected by the destruction raging outside. On a closer look, *Ajatshatru* could make out that someone had entered the huts and had searched them. Help me! a terrible shriek rendered the atmosphere. It was coming from the middle of the forest which was the worst affected part in the whole valley. Someone please help me; the voice echoed again. It was the voice of a desperate person filled with fear and panic. *Ajatshatru* had no other choice but to enter the forest and rescue the person in distress.

The going became difficult with each passing step. The fire had ravaged the entire forest and was fast moving towards the lake. The ground under *Ajatshatru*'s feet had become so hot that his each step resulted in big blisters on his feet. He was finding it difficult to breathe. The smoke was entering his lungs and choking him. His eyes were smarting and visibility was negligible. Help me! The sound of distress was coming from nearby. *Ajatshatru* inched slowly towards the place from where the sound was coming from. Deep inside, in the middle of the forest, *Ajatshatru* reached a small clearing and was startled to see a boy sitting in the middle with his face covered, surrounded by fire from all sides and crying for help.

Don't worry, I will rescue you, *Ajatshatru* shouted as soon he saw the boy. The boy uncovered his face and with large blue eyes looked at him, a sigh of relief on his face. The moment *Ajatshatru* looked at the boy, the ground suddenly gave way beneath his feet. Staring at him was *Satvik*, his friend whom he had seen dead and buried neck deep with face mutilated and the alchemy symbol of decay branded on his head. *Satvik*, he said and rushed forward to save his friend. *Satvik*'s face lit up as soon as he spotted *Ajatshatru* and he started sobbing uncontrollably. Where have you been till now, he spoke between sobs. That fateful night, I and *Moti* left to fetch some food but got lost in the forest. It was raining very heavily and a branch fell down on me and knocked me unconscious. When I woke up, there was no sign of *Moti*. I have been wondering in the forest ever since. After crossing several ridges, I reached this place and was just starting to explore it when the fire started. Had you not heard my cries, I would have been long dead by now.

Ajatshatru was moved beyond words. All along it was his dear friend who had got lost and had somehow stumbled onto the mysterious valley creating a scare amongst the members of the secret society. But who was the person whose mutilated body he had discovered in the forest, *Ajatshatru* wondered. Do not worry, he said. I am coming to rescue you. Saying this, he rushed forward towards *Satvik* without caring about the tall flames which were now licking every part of his body and had singed his hair. Come dear friend *Ajatshatru,* save me from this terrible fire before it completely devours me, *Satvik* shouted.

Ajatshatru reached *Satvik* who was now struggling to get up from the ground. He was terribly burnt and was hardly able to stand up. The flames had burnt most of his body and skin was peeling away from his face, legs and arms exposing his flesh and bones. Oh poor *Satvik*, *Ajatshatru* exclaimed and in one scoop lifted him off the ground and into his arms. I will not let you die, he said.

Suddenly *Satvik* turned around to face *Ajatshatru*. His burnt face had a hint of a cruel smile. Before

Ajatshatru could realize, *Satvik* threw burning red hot embers which he had hidden in his hands into *Ajatshatru*'s eyes. Aaah! *Ajatshatru* exclaimed, hurling *Satvik* onto the ground and instinctively covering his eyes with both his eyes. His eyes had melted under the impact of the red hot embers and the pain was so excruciating that it numbed his entire body and was sending it into a state of shock and cardiac arrest. Oh my friend, what have you done... *Ajatshatru* shouted.

The heinous laugh of *Satvik* reverberated along the entire valley. It was pure unadulterated evil. No longer was *Satvik* the innocent young boy who had followed *Ajatshatru* and was his constant companion and friend. The person standing before *Ajatshatru* was a scheming devil full of hatred and anger. *Ajatshatru*'s cries of pain were sending waves of joy and excitement down *Satvik*'s spine. The entire scene was shocking and unbelievable. Standing in the middle of a burning forest was a badly burnt boy laughing at the excruciating pain caused to his savior by the burning embers which he had thrown into the man's eyes by deceit and treachery.

You thought that you could get away from me, *Satvik* growled. I was there all along your journey; following you like your own shadow. I was there at Allahabad when you ran away from me at the *ghat*; I was there during your journey to *Kailash Mansarovar*; I was outside the cave when *Manu* was giving you sermon; I was there in *Haridwar* and in *Dharamsala*. You cannot escape from me, *Satvik* said between peals of laughter. The searing pain in *Ajatshatru*'s eyes was getting unbearable. It seemed as if his eyes had melted away leaving behind two hollow sockets inside which someone had inserted two live wires which were electrocuting his brain.

The time has come for you to bid farewell to your life, my friend. The words slowly floated inside *Ajatshatru*'s ears. He was breathing heavily and slipping in and out of consciousness. Relax; the words suddenly jolted *Ajatshatru* back into consciousness. It was almost a lifetime ago when he had heard the soothing and magical voice of *Manu Rishi*. Oh my savior; he cried, the pain suddenly seeming insignificant to the calm and caressing voice of the *Rishi*. Remember, the body is just a vehicle to take you from one place to another and obey your wishes, the *Rishi* said. You are not the body. You are invincible; a part of this magnificent creation. You cannot be harmed; you cannot be killed; fire cannot burn you and water cannot drown you. You were there from times immemorial and you will be there for times to come. Don't be fooled by sensations. Rise above them. Mind always leads and the body follows. You are the master of your body; it will obey you till the very last. Get up and fight. Do your duty. Rest will follow, *Manu Rishi*'s words echoed in *Ajatshatru*'s ears.

Aah, *Ajatshatru* cried. *Satvik* had stabbed him in the heart with a sharp and pointed branch. It was deeply stuck inside his lungs and he suddenly started coughing blood. Gasping for breath, *Ajatshatru* turned around to face *Satvik*. He was blind. He had no idea about *Satvik*'s location. In addition, his lungs were collapsing. *Ajatshatru* realized that he now had limited breaths before his lungs gave way and collapsed. His body had suffered tremendous damage and would die in a few moments.

Ajatshatru focused inwards. He commanded his body to breathe for few more moments till such time his mission was fulfilled. He concentrated and slowly his soul rose from within and left his body attached to it with the spiritual thread. *Ajatshatru* was free; liberated from the limitations of his body. He could clearly see *Satvik* standing in front of his dying body with a wicked smile on his face; the burning forest all around; the lake; surrounding ridges and the entire planet. The time for action had come.

With a huge roar, *Ajatshatru* suddenly stood up and with superhuman strength lifted *Satvik* off the ground and smashed his head on a protruding rock. In a moment, life was snatched out of *Satvik*; his body lifeless with skull shattered and brain splattered on the ground. Suddenly, as if by miracle, it started raining. *Ajatshatru* collapsed on the ground, lifeless.

Epilogue

It was a bright sunny day. The cool breeze was rustling against his face and the sweet melody of a thousand birds chirping filled his ears. There was lush greenery as far as his eyes could see and sweet scent of spring filled the air. *Ajatshatru* felt as if his complete being; each cell and molecule was filled with joy and harmony. There was complete bliss.

So how was your first adventure son, *Manu Rishi* asked? *Ajatshatru*, *Manu Rishi* and *Rishi Kripal* were sitting cross legged on the grass enjoying the beauty of nature. There were no scars on him. He was able to see. There was no pain. All three of them were dressed in flowing white robes and as far as his eyes could see there was no one in sight.

It was a real challenge, *Ajatshatru* replied. I never could imagine that such a young and innocent boy could have so much anger and hate bottled inside him. We all tend to get swayed by external appearances and display of emotions, *Rishi Kripal* replied. What lies beneath is the actual essence which needs to be discovered and analyzed. Sometimes in life, the staunchest perceived enemy help out the most, while the best friend stabs in the back. You displayed exceptional qualities of compassion and courage and we are proud of you, *Manu Rishi* said.

But I could not understand how *Pisach* could follow me all along my journey, *Ajatshatru* asked. Our minds are our mirrors to the outside world. Reading minds is not impossible. You can master the art of reading minds like you have mastered the art of breath control or astral travel. *Pisach* was continuously reading your mind and then sending his followers behind you, *Rishi Kripal* answered.

Where am I, *Ajatshatru* asked? I feel no pain. There are no scars, no injuries, no burn marks, nothing. I can see everything, feel everything and above all I am filled with tremendous love and joy as if my whole being will break into a joyous song right away. I have never felt like this before in my entire life, he added. You are experiencing the pure state of bliss, my son, *Manu Rishi* said. Achieving this state in a lifetime is very difficult. People spend years and lifetimes in prayers and devotion just to experience a moment of this state. This is the ultimate state of *Nirvan*. There is no beginning, no end. Time as a dimension does not exist here. There is no decay, no entropy. There is nothing left to achieve. Nothing left to desire. Everything is here yet there is nothing, he further added.

What about the alchemy team; are they safe, Ajatshatru asked? The team is absolutely safe, *Manu Rishi* replied. Thanks to your valiant efforts, the team's secrets are safe. But the valley is no longer safe for them. They have been successfully relocated to a different part of the world with their precious cargo. They have to start afresh. It is a big setback, but they have overcome such setbacks earlier and will overcome it again.

Am I dead, *Ajatshatru* asked with a quizzical expression on his face. The serious tone and expression of *Ajatshatru* sent both, *Manu Rishi* and *Rishi Kripal* into peals of laughter. After a while, *Rishi Kripal* replied. *Ajatshatru*, the soul sitting right amongst us is as much alive as we both are. In fact you have never been more alive than this moment during your entire life. The mortal body that was your temporary home for the past twenty two years is long dead and one with the mother earth. It had served its purpose. But till the time the secret of the sacred teams exists, your purpose remains.

I have not understood, *Ajatshatru* said. Son, replied *Manu Rishi*. You have a mission to fulfill. The secret teams are under constant threat from *Pisach*. You have been successful in only eliminating one of its followers. You have been chosen as the eternal guardian of the secret teams. Till such time the secret is not shared with humanity, you will continue to roam Earth in one form or the other. We will always be there to assist you in your task.

You mean to say that I have been reborn as a different human being; *Ajatshatru* asked his eyes growing big with surprise. The saints smiled. We have given you the power to remember your previous births so that you don't have to rediscover yourself like previous time, *Rishi Kripal* said. However, be careful not to disclose your knowledge to anyone. All your powers and memory will be instantaneously taken away as soon as you disclose your secret.

I will never disclose my secret to anyone, *Ajatshatru* said. Well son, the time has come to bid goodbye for the time being. Remember, *Pisach* is out there and is gaining strength with each passing moment. Always stay alert and stay prepared, said *Rishi Kripal*. I will my master, *Ajatshatru* replied.

The piece of chalk struck *Hirohito* with full force on his face, suddenly jolting him out of his trance. All around him, the students of his class were screaming in delight while the class teacher was staring down at him with utter disgust and disdain. How many times I have told you not to sleep in the class, she screamed. Sorry madam, *Hirohito* replied, a thin smile spreading across his face.